SNAKE POEMS

An Aztec Invocation

Francisco X. Alarcón

To
Eryn
Nomatca Nehuatl
All the power
to you—
from a poet
in flames—

Francisco X. Alarcón
July 21, 1994

CHRONICLE BOOKS
SAN FRANCISCO

ACKNOWLEDGMENTS:

Special thanks to Andrés Segura, tireless *maestro* of the *Mexica-Tenochca* tradition, the present and former members of *El Centro Chicano/Latino de Escritores* of the San Francisco Bay Area for their constant support and personal encouragement, and the *Rhythmagics* of Santa Cruz, who have brought music and percussion to my life.

Poems from this collection have previously appeared in the following publications: *The Americas Review*: "Cutting Wood," "To Earthworms Before Fishing with a Hook," "Chicome-Coatl: Seven Snake," "For Planting Camotes," "To Undo the Sleep Spell"; *The Bloomsbury Review*: "Matriarch"; *City on a Hill*: "Traveler's Prayer"; *Five Fingers Review*: "Four Directions," "Hernando Ruiz de Alarcón"; *Guadalupe Review*: "Tonalamatl," "Little Toltecs," "Rainbow," "Canto a las tortillas," "To Cast Sleep," "Seer," "Reconciling"; *High Plains Literary Review*: "Herbs"; *New Chicano Writing*: "Silence"; *Puerto del Sol*: "Drought"; *Poetry USA*: "Against Unruly Ants," "Midnight Water Song," "Visions"; *Quarry West*: "Birds," "Domingo Hernández"; *Red Dirt*: "Against Anger," "Martín de Luna"; *Tonantzin*: "For Planting Corn"; *ZYZZYVA*: "Mestizo," "Ollin: Movement," "Ode to Tomatoes."

Printed in The United States of America

LIBRARY OF CONGRESS CATALOGING-IN-PUBLICATION DATA
Alarcón, Francisco X., 1954–
    Snake poems : an Aztec invocation / by Francisco X. Alarcón.
    p.   cm.
    Includes bibliographical references.
    ISBN 0-8118-0161-6
    1. Aztecs—Religion and mythology—Poetry.
  2. Indians of Mexico—Religion and mythology—Poetry.
  3. Ruiz de Alarcón, Hernando—Poetry.   I. Title.
  PS3551.L22S64 1992
  811'.54—dc20   91-30469
                                        CIP

Distributed in Canada by Raincoast Books,
112 East Third Avenue, Vancouver, B.C. V5T 1C8

10 9 8 7 6 5 4 3 2 1

Chronicle Books
275 Fifth St.
San Francisco, CA 94103

To all the Earth keepers!

. . . ye no taamiqui
no titeocihui . . .

. . . now you're very thirsty
and also hungry . . .

Martín de Luna

Contents

Before These Poems, and After

This present collection is something much more than just another new volume by a contemporary poet. For as new as *Snake Poems* is, it is bound inextricably to the past. It is like the serpent of fire that opens up its mouth to meet its double at the center of the exterior ring of the Sun Stone known as the Aztec Calendar. This text by Californian poet Francisco X. Alarcón is an encounter with another text completed in 1629 by one Hernando Ruiz de Alarcón, a Catholic parish priest from Atenango, a small town in the present state of Guerrero, Mexico.

The poetry of *Snake Poems* emerges as an encounter with the colonial manuscript on Native American beliefs by Ruiz de Alarcón, *Tratado de las supersticiones y costumbres gentílicas que oy viven entre los indios naturales desta Nueva España* (Treatise on the Superstitions and Heathen Customs That Today Live Among the Indians Native to This New Spain). Ruiz de Alarcón labored more than ten years compiling, translating and interpreting the Nahuatl spells and invocations. The only extant copy of the handwritten *Tratado* is now found in the Museo Nacional de Antropología in Mexico City.

Ruiz de Alarcón's *Tratado* was compiled a hundred years after the Spanish conquest of Mexico and remains one of the most important sources on Native religion, beliefs and medicine. Its importance lies in the spells, curing practices, and myths that were transcribed in the original Nahuatl, the language of the Aztecs. It is this language transcription that allows so much of the original speakers to come to us today. And this is despite the compiler's insidious intent. Simply stated, Ruiz de Alarcón wrote on a mission for God, to expose heathen practice among the Indians and to extend the repressive practice of the Spanish Inquisition in Mexico. To gather the raw data for his catalog of practices, the author did not stop short of torturing his informants. Ruiz de

Alarcón was admonished for his over-zealous interview techniques and yet was able to finish his work undisturbed, and, ironically, promoted to ecclesiastical judge because of the extreme zeal of his faith.

Francisco X. Alarcón's poems reflect the world view and belief systems of Indians in Mexico three and a half centuries ago. But clearly, *Snake Poems* is poetry, not ethnography, and the reflection it casts of the *Tratado* is nowhere near a mirror image. It is good that this is so. The poems are poems that stand as such, completely on their own. What Francisco X. Alarcón has captured in *Snake Poems* from *Tratado* is the spirit of the Indian informants, a sense of Native culture alive despite the best efforts to misread and suppress it.

Commentators on the *Tratado* frequently mention Ruiz de Alarcón's poor translation and weak evaluation of some spells in Nahuatl, which seem only guided by his religious prejudice and cultural bias. Francisco X. Alarcón reads *through* the *Tratado,* past the surface prepared for the Inquisition, down to the living speakers whose spells and chants and beliefs are recorded, down to Martín de Luna, Mariana, Domingo Hernández, Magdalena Pretronila Xochiquetzal, and other named Indians. And while their words can only come by way of Ruiz de Alarcón, *Snake Poems* reflects the gaps, the lacunae, the interstices of cultural survival.

All quotations and references that appear in *Snake Poems* come directly from Ruiz de Alarcón's *Tratado*, with five very telling exceptions. There is an invocation by Mazatec curandera María Sabina, and a quote from New Mexican weaver Agueda Martínez. There is allusion to living poets, to the Chicanos Tino Villanueva and Lucha Corpi, and the Nicaraguan poet, priest, and former Sandinista Minister of Culture Ernesto Cardenal. For Francisco X. Alarcón, the snake poems are very much alive: Mesoamerican consciousness survives not only in the collective memory but also in the live words of the descendants of the original Indian authors. So while the poem "Mestizo" celebrates the many strands that meet and hybridize in New World people, the epigraph by Agueda Martínez grounds identity very clearly, "*ya que sea seamos hispanos, mexicanos; semos más indios*": more than Hispanics or Mexicans, we are Indians.

There are 104 *Snake Poems,* not an arbitrary number but one chosen for its significance in Native thought. One hundred and four is twice the fifty-two-year cycle of the Mesoamerican calendar. It is as if one cycle occurred in the first translation of Nahuatl thought, Ruiz de Alarcón's *Tratado,* and the second cycle occurs now with *Snake Poems.* The first section of *Snake Poems,* "Tahui," contains twenty poems, one for each day of the Mesoamerican month. The final section, "New Day," contains six poems, alluding to the new era of the Sixth Sun.

The poems are spare in line-length and in language; nothing is wasted; very much is said. On the page, some of the poems appear long and lean like serpents on the desert floor. And there are the illustrations that somehow seem as much at home beside English and Spanish as they do beside Nahuatl. Beside the epigraph of Tino Villanueva's invocation to Tlacuilo, there is the image of the writer, the speaker, making words. Image and form intertwine with the voices and the languages of the past and the present: a poetics of ancient oral magic and modern verse. *Snake Poems* is alive with a simultaneously present and past passion and concern; it brims with the spirit of those who sang despite the fact that their very songs could lead to punishment and death.

Read these poems as expressions of life, as a celebration of the Native heritage of *Mestizo* America. Some poems uplift and some are humorous, and when taken together, they sing in collective spirit, vigorous, denying death. And then stop reading, put your ear to the page and hear the faint yet persistent echoes. I do.

Alfred Arteaga
English Department
University of California, Berkeley

Author's Note

The only extant manuscript copy of Hernando Ruiz de Alarcón's *Tratado de las supersticiones y costumbres gentílicas que oy viven entre los indios naturales desta Nueva España, 1629,* is in the library of the Museo Nacional de Antropología in Mexico City. This manuscript has a total of 109 folio pages and includes 73 different chapters divided among 6 main treatises. Not all of the Nahuatl spells in the *Tratado* appear in *Snake Poems*—only some of the most representative spells have been selected. The Spanish texts by Ruiz de Alarcón have been rendered according to the contemporary spelling of modern standard Spanish.

Diacritics have been omitted in the Nahuatl transcriptions, which generally follow the scholarly texts done by J. Richard Andrews and Ross Hassig (1984). The main departure from the work of these two fine linguists is my decision to follow the position taken by the late Mexican scholar Angel María Garibay Kintana and align the spells as poems.

Many of the Nahuatl spells have several—sometimes differing—translations available in various European languages; these texts have been included in the bibliography. The parallel translations into English have taken into consideration all the previous translations into Spanish and English—but the author is solely responsible for any deficiency in this endeavor. The numerals provided before spells document the treatise and chapter where they originally appeared.

The designs on the subtitle pages are taken from a book on pre-Hispanic Mexican stamps by Frederick V. Field (1974). The other illustrations that appear throughout the text come from Mesoamerican monuments and Indian codices and are reproductions from two very insightful works by Laurette Sejourné (1962 and 1984).

PRONUNCIATION OF THE NAHUATL SPELLS

There are only four vowels in Nahuatl (*a, e, i, o*). The "*u*" sound is a consonant. Nahuatl vowels resemble their equivalents in Spanish. Although long and short vowels have been recognized in Nahuatl, due to the inconsistencies in the *Tratado* regarding the use of diacritics marking the length of vowels, only a single value has been assigned to vowels in the spelling of the Nahuatl spells. For a more ample discussion on the pronunciation and standard spelling of Nahuatl refer to Andrews and Hassig (1984).

Since the spelling of Nahuatl using the Roman alphabet was first introduced by Franciscan missionaries in the 16th century, Spanish orthography has served as a general guide for the transcription of Nahuatl sounds. An exception to this rule is the letter "*x*," which is pronounced like *sh* in *ship*. Stress usually falls on the next-to-the-last syllable. There are no diphthongs in Nahuatl. Two adjacent vowels fall in separate syllables. The diagraph letters (*ch, tl, tz, hu, uh, cu,* and *uc*) are considered single letters, therefore *atlan* is pronounced *a-tlan*; and *chiucnahui, chiuc-na-hui*. Two adjacent consonants are always divided: *axcan* and *calli* are pronounced *ax-can* and *cal-li*, respectively.

Lo cierto es que las más o casi todas las adoraciones actuales o acciones idolátricas, que ahora hallamos, y a lo que podemos juzgar, son las mismas que acostumbraban sus antepasados, tienen su raíz y fundamento formal en tener ellos fe que las nubes son ángeles y dioses, capaces de adoración, y lo mismo juzgan a los vientos, por lo cual creen que en todas las partes de la tierra habitan como en las lomas, montes, valles y quebradas. Lo mismo creen de los ríos, lagunas y manantiales, pues a todo lo dicho ofrecen cera e incienso.

What is certain is that most or almost all present-day forms of worship or idolatrous actions which we now come across (and, from what we can judge, they are the same ones their ancestors customarily used) have their roots and formal basis in their belief that the clouds are angels and gods worthy of worship. They think the same of the winds since they believe these forces live everywhere, in the hills, mountains, valleys, and ravines. They believe the same of the rivers, lakes, and springs, since they offer wax and incense to all the above.

Hernando Ruiz de Alarcón, Treatise on the Superstitions and Heathen Customs That Today Live Among the Indians Native to This New Spain, 1629.

TAHUI

Los flecheros llaman cuatro veces a los
venados, repitiendo cuatro veces esta
palabra tahui, *que hoy no hay quien la*
entienda, y luego gritan cuatro veces
a semejanza de león.

The archers call four times to the
deer, repeating four times this word
tahui which nobody understands
today, and then they cry out four
times like a puma.

Ruiz de Alarcón (I:2)

Hello

tahui
tahui
tahui
tahui

Four Directions

West

we are
salmons
looking for
our womb

North

eagles
flying
the Sun
in our beak

East

coyotes
calling
each other
in the Moon

South

we turn
into snakes
by eating
chile

Silence

I smell
silence
everywhere

clean
nice homes
smell

banks
smell
so do malls

no deodorant
odorizer
or perfume

can put away
this stink
of silence

Hernando Ruiz de Alarcón

(1587–1646)

eras tú	it was you
al que buscabas	you were looking for
Hernando	Hernando
hurgando	searching
en los rincones	every house
de las casas	corner
semillas	for some
empolvadas	dusty seeds
de ololiuhqui	of *ololiuhqui*
eras tú	it was you
al que engañabas	whom you tricked
y aprehendías	and apprehended
eras tú	it was you
el que preguntaba	who both questioned
y respondía	and responded
dondequiera	everywhere
mirabas moros	you saw Moors
con trinchete	with long knives
y ante	and in front of
tanto dolor	so much sorrow
tanta muerte	so much death
un conquistador	you became
conquistado	a conquered
fuiste	conqueror

sacerdote	priest
soñador	dreamer
cruz parlante	speaking cross
condenando	condemning
te salvaste	you saved yourself
al transcribir	by transcribing
acaso	maybe
sin saber	without knowing
el cielo	the heavens
soy yo	I am
el de tu cepa	from your tree
el de tu sueño	from your dream
este cenzontle	this *cenzontle* bird
del monte:	in the wilderness:
tu mañana	your tomorrow

Same

we see
feel   taste
are so
differently
the same

In the Middle of the Night

sobs
woke me

I got up
and saw

myself
in a corner

crying

I'm Not Really Crying

it's just
the sheer
number
of chopped
onions
in the world

Shame

I washed
my arms
scrubbed
my face

powdered
soap
fell from
my hands

but
my skin
only got
redder

I was
just
another
itching

brown
boy
getting
ready

for school

Mestizo

my name
is not
Francisco

there is
an Arab
within me

who prays
three times
each day

behind
my Roman
nose

there is
a Phoenician
smiling

my eyes
still see
Sevilla

but
my mouth
is Olmec

my dark
hands are
Toltec

my cheekbones
fierce
Chichimec

my feet
recognize
no border

no rule
no code
no lord

for this
wanderer's
heart

Matriarch

my dark
grandmother

would brush
her long hair

seated out
on her patio

even ferns
would bow

to her splendor
and her power

Rescue

at the end
I found

myself
holding

the other end
of the rope

Tonalamatl / Spirit Book

pages
whisper
sigh
sing

glyphs
dance
left
to right

I follow
the drums
the scent
the stairs

mountain
mist
sprays
my hair

I learn
to undo
what is
done

an ancient
jaguar
roars at
my face

I start
singing
all kinds
of flowers

Songs

xochitl
flower
flor

Nahual

this whale
can't stop
singing
from
the bottom
of the sea

Ollin / Movement

I call myself
waterfall

Quetzalcoatl
spirit and flesh

Xolotl
his twin

Oxomoco
the first man

Cipactonal
the first woman

the couple *Tlaloc*
and *Xochiquetzal*

Centeotl, their kid
and popcorn . . .

I go on calling
names

keep hearing
my mirror

To Those Who Have
Lost Everything

crossed
in despair
many deserts
full of hope

carrying
their empty
fists of sorrow
everywhere

mouthing
a bitter night
of shovels
and nails

"you're nothing
you're shit
your home's
nowhere":

mountains
will speak
for you

rain
will flesh
your bones

green again
among ashes
after a long fire

started in
a fantasy island
some time ago

turning
Natives
into aliens

Never Alone

always
this caressing
Wind

this Earth
whispering
to our feet

this boundless
desire
of being

grass
tree
corazón

Heart

fragrant
flower
open at
midnight

Temicxoch

in my sleep
I smell
the roots
of this flower

Nomatca Nehuatl

I myself:
the mountain
the ocean
the breeze
the flame

the thorn
the serpent
the feather
the Moon
the Sun

the sister
the brother
the mother
the father
the other

the ground
the seed
the chant
the cloud
the flower

the deer
the hunter
the arrow
the neck
the blood

the dead
the dancing
the house
the quake
the lizard

the island
the shell
the collar
the star
the lover

the search
the face
the dream
the heart
the voice:

nomatca nehuatl!

INCANTATIONS
SPELLS
INVOCATIONS

Vigila por mí, Tlacuilo venerable,
ayúdame a ser fiel a mi linaje, las flechas
castigadas por el sol y lavadas por la sombra.
Bendíceme, dile a tus dioses que oren por mí . . .

Look after me, venerable Tlacuilo,
help me to be true to my ancestors, arrows
scorched by the Sun and bathed by Darkness.
Bless me, tell your gods to pray for me . . .

Tino Villanueva

1. Penitents

Midnight Water Song

the eagle's
wing is
my fan

my people's
past is
my staff

my pounding
heart
the only drum

this nightfall
this sagebrush
this cedar smoke

tumbleweeds
rattle
as I sing

of peyote's
flowering rain
in the desert

Journey

Ruiz de Alarcón (I:4)

In each village there was a large, well-kept courtyard, something like a church, from where the *tlamacazqui,* the old priest, would send the *tlamaceuhque,* the penitent, on his rite of passage. Each individual began his pilgrimage by bringing green firewood to this courtyard for the elders, who were distinguished by a long lock of hair. This lock of hair was also a sign among Indians of great captains and warriors called *tlacauhque.*

During the night, the elder, squatting on a low stone seat and holding in his hands a large *tecomate,* "gourd vessel," full of *tenex yhetl,* "tobacco with lime," would then address the *tlamaceuhque,* ordering him to go to the forest, home of *Tlalticpaque,* Lord of the Wilderness. The words the elder spoke were:

xoniciuhtiuh	hurry off
nocomichic	bottom of my vessel
noxocoyo	my youngest child
noceuhteuh	my only one
mazan cana	beware of delaying
timaahuiltitiuh	somewhere—
nimitzchixtiyez	I'll be watching you
nican niyetlacuitica	here smoking my tobacco pipe
nitlacuepalotica	keeping up the fire
nitlachixtica	I'm watching you
izca	behold!—
nimitzcualtia	I give you
tichuicaz . . .	food to carry . . .
nican nitlachixtica	here I'm watching you—
nOxomoco	I, *Oxomoco*
niHuehueh	I, the Ancient One
niCipactonal	I, *Cipactonal*

Traveler's Prayer

Ruiz de Alarcón (II:1)

nomatca nehuatl	I myself
niQuetzalcoatl	I, Quetzalcoatl
niMatl	I, the Hand
ca nehuatl niYaotl	indeed I, the Warrior
niMoquequeloatzin	I, the Mocker
atle ipan nitlamati . . .	I respect nothing . . .
tla xihualhuian	come forth
tlamacazque	spirits
tonatiuh iquizayan	from the sunset
tonatiuh icalaquiyan	from the sunrise
in ixquichca nemi	anywhere you dwell
in yolli	as animals
in patlantinemi	as birds
in ic nauhcan	from the four directions
niquintzatzilia	I call you
ic axcan yez . . .	to my grip . . .
tla xihuallauh	come forth
Ce-Tecpatl	knife
tezzohuaz	to be stained
titlapallohuaz	with blood
tla xihuallauh	come forth
Tlaltecuin	cross my path

35

Martín de Luna

Martín de Luna
110 years old
was arrested
and imprisoned

for having used
incantations
before laying down
on his *petate:*

"*tla cuel
nocelopetlatzine
in nauhcampa
ticamachalohtoc* . . .

"*take me
jaguar mat into
the four mouths
of your corners* . . ."

(*take me now
from this cell
and lose me
in the darkness*)

Day and Night

I bleed
in silence
all alone

Martín
Mariana
Domingo

in fields
in streets
in cells

my fists
hit
walls

whips
undress
my ribs

from
my mouth
come out

broken teeth
blood
butterflies

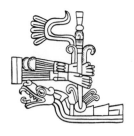

En el pueblo de Iguala, haciendo yo pesquisa de estos delitos por orden y mandato del Illmo. Sr. D. Juan de la Serna, Arzobispo de México, el año pasado de seiscientos y diez y siete, prendí una india llamada Mariana, sortílega, embustera, curandera de las que llaman Ticitl; esta Mariana declaró que lo que ella sabía y usaba de sus sortilegios y embustes, lo había aprendido de otra india, de Mariana su hermana, y que la dicha hermana no lo había aprendido de persona alguna, sino que le había sido revelado, porque consultando la dicha hermana al ololiuhqui sobre la cura de una llaga vieja, habiéndose embriagado con la fuerza de la bebida llamó al enfermo y sobre unas brasas le sopló la llaga, con que luego sanó la llaga, y tras el soplo inmediatamente se le apareció un mancebo que juzgó ser ángel y la consoló diciéndole: "no tengas pena, cata aquí, te da Dios una gracia y dádiva porque vives pobre y en mucha miseria, para que con esta gracia tengas chile y sal,

Last year, 1617, while by order and mandate of the Most Reverend Don Juan de la Serna, Archbishop of Mexico, I was investigating certain crimes in the village of Iguala, I arrested an Indian woman named Mariana— a sorceress, charlatan, and healer of the kind they call Ticitl. This Mariana declared she had learned the sorceries and tricks she practiced from her sister. The sister had learned them from no one; they had been revealed to her when consulting the ololiuhqui about the cure of an old wound. Having become intoxicated with the force of the drink, she summoned the sick person and blew on the wound over some hot coals, healing it immediately. Following this cure, there appeared to her a youth whom she judged to be an angel. He consoled her, saying: "Don't worry. Behold, God is granting you a favor and a gift because you live in poverty and misery. Through this favor you will have chile and salt (that is to say,

quiere decir, sustento: curarás las llagas, con sólo lamerlas, y el sarpullido y viruelas, y si no acudieres a esto, morirás"; y tras esto estuvo el dicho mancebo toda la noche dándole una cruz, y crucificándola en ella y clavándole clavos en las manos, y estando dicha india en la cruz, el mancebo le enseñó los modos que sabía de curar, que eran siete o más exorcismos e invocaciones, y que tuvieron quince días continuos luz donde estaba el enfermo de la llaga dicha: debió de ser en veneración de la cura y del portento.

sustenance). You will cure sores, rashes, and smallpox just by licking them. And if you don't answer this call, you will die."
The youth gave her a cross, and stayed the night hammering nails through her hands. Then, while the Indian woman was on the cross, he taught her the seven or more exorcisms and incantations he knew for curing. Following this, there were fifteen continuous days of light where the patient with the wound was— this had to be in veneration of the cure and the portent.

Ruiz de Alarcón (I:7)

Yolloxochitl / Heart-Flower

it was you
sister
your voice
a seagull
holding up
the breeze

it was you
sister
your breath
forming
tiny tears
on windows

it was you
your ways
to climb down
crosses
turn things
around

it was you
your hands
that healed
mended
the sick
the needy

it was you
sister
your blood
your wounds

Ololiuhqui

to Bárbara García

seeds
of wisdom
divine eyes
of serpents

teach us
to read
again
the sky

buttons of
the infinite
skirt
of stars

turn us
into
hummingbirds
kissing flowers

lead us
back
to the lap
of our Mother

2. Hunters

Morning Ritual

I fold
kiss
carry

my life
inside
my pocket

Sucedió pues que viniendo a orillas de este río de mi beneficio un indio vecino del pueblo de Santiago, llamado Francisco de Santiago, alcanzó otros que se estaban bañando y pasando por ellos, vio en el camino un papel escrito, y cogiolo sin ser visto, y leyéndolo entendió lo que contenía, por haberse criado en mi casa; y así me trajo luego el papel y me refirió lo que contenía, cómo lo halló y cuyo era. Porque estaba firmado del dueño, que era un sacristán del pueblo de Cuetlaxxochitla, que apenas sabía escribir; mas el demonio le ayudó para que no se perdiese este maleficio. Traído el autor, confesó el delito y dijo habérsele perdido el original, de cuyo autor no supo dar razón.

One day when Francisco de Santiago, an Indian from the village of Santiago, arrived at the banks of a nearby river, he came upon others who were taking a bath. As he passed by them, he saw on the road a piece of paper with writing on it. He picked it up without being seen, and on examining it closer, understood its significance, since he had been reared in my house. He then brought me the paper, and told me what it contained, how he had found it and whose it was. It had been signed by a sacristan in the village of Cuetlaxxochitla who was hardly able to write, but whom the Devil had helped in order that this spell not be lost. When the signator was brought, he confessed the crime and said that he had lost the original, about whose author he could give no information.

Ruiz de Alarcón (II:4)

Prayer for the Sun Before Traveling

Ruiz de Alarcón (II:4)

tla cuel	come
tla xihualmohuica	help me
Nanahuatzin	Nanahuatzin
achtopa niyaz	I'll go first
achtopa notlatocaz	I'll be on the road first—
zatepan tiyaz	then you'll go
zatepan totlatocaz	then you'll follow the road
achtopa nictlamiltiz	I'll be the first to cross
in centeotlalotli	all the desert lands
in cencomolihuic	all the canyon lands
ca ye niquiczaz	I'll pass swiftly over
in Tlalli Ixcapactzin	the Earth's smooth face—
ahmo nechelehuiz	she won't hinder me
ca ahmo nelli	no matter what truly lies
Tlalli Ixcapactzin	on her smooth face:
ca zan ilhuicac	up in the sky
ipan nonyaz	I shall go
ipan ninemiz	I shall walk

Cutting Wood

ahmo
tinechelehuiliz

tree
don't hurt my ax

enjoy it
as your mirror

I offer tobacco
for your shin

Birds

snakes
in flight

For Hunting Birds

Ruiz de Alarcón (II:6)

nomatca nehuatl	I myself
nIcnopiltzintli	I, Poor Orphan
niCenteotl	I, *Centeotl*
niQuetzalcoatl	I, *Quetzalcoatl*
onihualla niquintemoz	I've come to seek
in notlahuan	my uncles
tlamacazque	the spirits
ilhuicac pipiltin	the nobles of the sky
tlaca ye nican oneque	but already sitting here
in notlahuan	are my uncles
tlamacazque	the spirits
Olchipinque	*Olchipinque*
Olpeyauhque	*Olpeyauhque*
nican nicualhuica	here I bring
in nonan ical	my mother's house
ihuipil	her *huipil*
nica nicehualtiz	here I shall place
in tlamacazqui	the priest
Ce-Atl Itonal	spirit One Water
itozcatlan	it shall enter
ixillan	the throat
iciacatlan	the belly
noconaquiz	the armpits
in nonan	of my mother
Chalchiuhcueye	*Chalchiuhcueye*
nican niquimonchiaz	here I shall wait
in notlahuan	for my uncles
tlamacazque	the spirits
Olchipinque	*Olchipinque*
Olpeyauhque	*Olpeyauhque*

Little Toltecs

"bees are
godly
servants
of the flowers

they keep
to themselves

they make
the wax
we burn
to our Lord

for that
we love them
we revere them"

said Miguel
the bee seeker
after being
tricked to recite

the incantations
of the beehives
he knew better
than his Ave Marías

For Hunting Deer

Ruiz de Alarcón (II:9)

ye nonehua nehuatl	I'm leaving
nIcnopiltzintli	I, Poor Orphan
niCenteotl	I, *Centeotl*
ye nichuica	carrying with me
Ce-Atl Itonal	the spirit One Water
yehuatl ihuan	his bow
iacayo	his arrows
in oquichichiuh	made by
in nonan	my mother
Tonacacihuatl	*Tonacacihuatl*
Xochiquetzal	*Xochiquetzal*
cihuatl	the woman
ompa icatiuh	who wears
itzapapalotl	obsidian butterflies
yequene eh nichuicaz	I shall carry back
nota Chicome-Xochitl	my father Seven Flower
Piltzinteuctli	Young Lord—
nicanaco	I've come to take him
nichuicaz	I shall carry him back—
ye quichixcaca	already awaiting him
nonan Xochiquetzal	is my mother *Xochiquetzal*
nictemoco can	I've come to seek him
in comolihuic	in ravines
tepeyacatl	on mountain summits
campa teliuhqui	wherever
quitocatinemi	he goes

Piltzinteuctli	it's the Young Lord
Chicome-Xochitl	Seven Flower
nictemoco can mani	I've come to seek
ihuan nictemoco	I've come to seek
Mixcoacihuatl	*Mixcoatl's* Woman
in Acaxochtzin	and Reed Flower—
nichuicaz	that's who I shall carry back

Ensnared Deer

Ruiz de Alarcón (II:8)

tlamazcaqui	spirit
Chicome-Xochitl	Seven Flower
teotlalhua	desert dweller
ye iuhqui	it's all over with
otititlanihuac	you're a goner
yohualli	in the night
can in	where is
Chicome-Xochitl	Seven Flower
can ca?	where is he?
ca opatoloc	and his luck?
ho ho!	ha ha!
tlamaloc	he was taken
ye iuhqui	it's all over with

Chicome-Xochitl / Seven Flower

deer
father

all
stems

pointing
stars

For Keeping Animals Out of Sown Fields

Ruiz de Alarcón (II:11)

As soon as the Indians get to the edge of the sown fields, they remove any broken stalks, ears of corn, spikes of grain or fallen fruit spoiled by the animals. Then, burning incense as an offering, they say:

nomatca nehuatl	I myself
niNahualocelotl	I, the Wizard Jaguar
onihualla niquimittaz	I've come to find
notlahuan	my uncles
tlamacazque	the spirits
cozauhque tlamacazque	the yellow spirits
yayauhque tlamacazque	the dark spirits
tlaca!	aha!
nican ohuallaque	here they came
tlaca!	aha!
nican ocalacque	here they entered
ye no nican quizque	and off they went
nican nihualla niquintotocaz	from here I chase them away
aocmo nican tlacuazque	they shall never eat here again
hueca niquintitlani	I'm sending them far off
hueca nemizque	and far off they shall stay
nican nichualhuica	here I bring forth
in iztac copalli	white copal
cozauhque copalli	yellow copal

ic niquintlacuiliz	with it I shall mark things away
in notlahuacan	from my uncles
tlamacazque	the spirits
cozauhque tlamacazque	the yellow spirits
yayauhque tlamacazque	the dark spirits
nota	o father
Nahuai-Acatl	Four Reed
Milintica	Flaming One!

Against Unruly Ants

Ruiz de Alarcón (II:13)

If the ants do not respond to the conjurer's pleas by leaving, he carries out his threat, destroying their houses by pouring a quantity of water onto the anthill and sprinkling the outer edge and circumference with his so venerated *piciete* ("tobacco").

tla cuel!	come now!
Chalchiuhcueye	Mother Water
tle in ai	what are the ants
in popotecatl?	doing around?
tla xiquimpopoloti	wipe them out
ahmo nechtlacamati	they don't obey me
cuiz nelhuayoticate?	are they perhaps
ye cuahuitl tichuica	rooted?
tictlalochtitiquiza	you uproot trees
in hueca ixtlahuacan	quickly wash them
teohixtlahuacan nepantla	away to the far-off
toconxiccahua	dusty plains
cuix annelhuayoticate?	are you perhaps rooted?
tla cuel!	come now!
Xoxouqui Tlamacazqui	Green Spirit
Xiuhpapatlantzin	Tobacco
tle axtica?	why delay more?
tla xocontocati	chase them away
in popotecatl	close their town

58

To Earthworms Before Fishing with a Hook

Ruiz de Alarcón (II:15)

tla xihualhuian	help me
in Iztac-Tlamacazqui	White Spirit
ye nican ihuan	soon here
timonahuahtequiz	you will embrace
in tlatlauhqui chichimecatl	the red chichimec
cuix zan ce nicnotza?	am I calling just one?
ca zan mochi nicnotza	indeed all of them I call:
in piltontli	the child fish
in huehuentzin	the man fish
ilamatzin	the woman fish—
in anenecuilcan chaneque	dwellers of meanders

Spirits of the Forest

when the last
rain forests
become zoos

will there be
lines to the pond
of wild dreams?

who will dare
disturb
this order of lies?

must the last
eagle die
in a cage?

what will take
the place of
our spirits?

3. Farmers

Quetzalcóatl, Codex Borbonicus

Sólo un dios tenían.
 Su nombre era Quetzalcóatl.
Su sacerdote,
 su nombre era también Quetzalcóatl.
Todo lo de Quetzalcóatl
 se los decía su sacerdote Quetzalcóatl:
Quetzalcóatl nada exige
 sino serpientes, sino mariposas
que vosotros debéis ofrecerle
 que vosotros debéis sacrificarle.

They only had one God.
 His name was Quetzalcóatl.
Their priest,
 his name was also Quetzalcóatl.
The priest Quetzalcóatl would tell them
 everything about Quetzalcóatl:
Quetzalcóatl demands nothing
 but serpents and butterflies,
which you must offer him
 which you must sacrifice to him.

Ancient Nahuatl poem quoted
in Quetzalcóatl *by Ernesto Cardenal*

First Offering

ourselves
molded out
of *huauhtli*

the first crop
smiling
everywhere

Aguamiel

in its heart
the *maguey*
weeps
sweats

streams
of sweet
tears
and drops

Clouds

mountains
dreaming
up the sky

De esta metáfora de las siete
culebras usan siempre en estos
conjuros por el maíz, y es o por los
racimos atados de las mazorcas, o
por las cañas en que se da, que de
ordinario los siembran y nacen de
siete en siete, o por las hileras del
maíz en la misma mazorca que
suelen asemejar las culebras
tendidas de diferentes colores.

This metaphor of the seven
snakes is always used in these
incantations for corn, and it
is either because of the tied
bunches of the ears or because of
the stalks on which it is pro-
duced, since they usually sow
them and they are born seven by
seven or because of the rows of
kernels on the ear which usually
resemble the snakes stretched
out in different colors.

Ruiz de Alarcón (III:2)

Chicome-Coatl / Seven Snake

corn stalks
are upright
snakes

corn ears
rattle
in the wind

Rueda víbora

habrá soy eres somos este futuro vuelto pasado todo lo que hubo hay

Snake Wheel

will be I you we are this future turned past all that once was is

Calendar Keepers

rattlesnakes
renew
themselves
each year

by shedding
their skins
by adding
a new ring

they trace
the shining
path of our
rainy seasons

Thunder

Tlaloc's
laughter

from
afar

Rainbow

seven
snakes

giving
thanks

Water Spirits

these rivers
flow deep
inside

well uphill
steam off
volcanoes

For Planting Corn

Ruiz de Alarcón (III:4)

nomatca nehuatl	I myself
nitlamacazqui	Spirit in Flesh:
tla xihualhuian	hear me, *Tonacacihuatl*
nohueltiuh	elder sister
Tonacacihuatl	Lady of Our Flesh
tla xihualhuian	hear me, *Tlalteuctli*
Tlalteuctli	Mother Earth
ye momacpalco	on your open hand
nocontlalia	I'm setting down
nohueltiuh	my elder sister
Tonacacihuatl	*Tonacacihuatl*
ahmo timopinauhtiz	don't shame yourself
ahmo tihuexcapehuaz	don't grumble
ahmo tihuexcatlatlacoz	don't laugh at us
cuix quin moztla	tomorrow
cuix quin huiptla	or the day after
in ixco icpac nitlachiaz	I want to see again
in nohueltiuh	the face of my elder sister
Tonacacihuatl	*Tonacacihuatl*
niman iciuhca	let her stand
in tlalticpac hualquizaz	on the ground
in nicmahuizoz	I shall greet
in nictlapaloz	I shall honor
in nohueltiuh	my elder sister
Tonacacihuatl	*Tonacacihuatl*

For Storing Corn

Ruiz de Alarcón (III:5)

nomatca nehuatl	I myself
nitlamacazqui	Spirit in Flesh:
tla xihualhuian	come forth
nohueltiuh	elder sister
Tonacacihuatl	Lady of Our Flesh
ye nimitzoncahuaz	soon I shall place you
in nochalchiuhcontzinco	inside my jade jar
nauhcampa xitlaquitzqui	hold up the four directions
ahmo timopinauhtiz	don't shame yourself
motech nihiyocuiz	you shall be my breath
motech niceceyaz	you shall be my cure
in nIcnopiltzintli	for me, Poor Orphan
in niCenteotl	for me, *Centeotl*
in tinohueltiuh	you, my elder sister
tiTonacacihuatl	you, *Tonacacihuatl*

For Planting *Camotes*

Ruiz de Alarcón (III:7)

This spell is spoken directly to the sun after the roots and stems have been prepared for planting.

nomatca nehuatl	I myself
nIcnopiltzintli	I, Poor Orphan
niCenteotl	I, *Centeotl:*
tla xihualhuian	come forth
notla	uncle
tlamacazqui Nanahuatzin	spirit *Nanahuatzin*
ca nican niquilpia	here I tie up
nometzcuauhyo	my thigh
nictoca	I plant it
tla xihualhuia	come forth
notla Nanahuatzin	uncle *Nanahuatzin*
ca nican niquilpia	here I tie up
notzontecon	my head
ca ica noconilpia	I tie it up
in nohueltiuh	to my sister
in tetencuacua xochitl	the lip-biting flower
temacochihuia xochitl	the embracing flower
itetzinco nihiouiz	with her I shall breathe
itetzinco nipahtiz	with her I shall heal
nicnotlacatzintli	I, just a poor person

Canto a las Tortillas

I go on
calling
nana to
the Earth

feeding on
the subversive
canto sown
by *los antiguos*

inside
the humblest
tortillas
of life

Ode to Tomatoes

they make
friends
anywhere

red
smiles
in salads

tender
young
generous

hot
salsa
dancers

round
cardinals
of the kitchen

hard
to imagine
cooking

without
first asking
their blessings!

Urban Villagers

hummingbirds
consoling
the flowers
of the avenues

Drought

despite
dry
years

siempre
verde
inside

4. Lovers

ya sea que seamos
hispanos, mexicanos;
semos más indios

whether we are
Hispanics, Mexicans;
we're really Indians

> *Agueda Martínez*
> *quoted in a film produced by*
> *filmmaker Moctezuma Esparza*

Potent Seeds

few corn
kernels
enough

to turn
anger
around

Una de las cosas de que usan por medicina a que atribuyen parte del efecto, son unos granos de maíz que tienen su asiento en principio y nacimiento de la espiga o mazorca, y tales granos tienen las puntillas contrarias al nacimiento, al revés y a la parte contraria que las demás de la dicha mazorca, y a esta contrariedad atribuyen el efecto contrario en la inclinación y voluntad en cuanto a la afición y odio. A estos granos de maíz aplican la segunda parte de este medio, que son las palabras con que a su juicio, conjurando los maíces, les dan nueva fuerza y virtud para conseguir el efecto del trueque que pretenden. . . . Hecho este conjuro para aplicar la medicina, moliendo el maíz conjurado, hacen de él alguna bebida al uso de esta tierra, como es atole y cacao, y dánselo a beber al que pretenden trueque la voluntad o afecto.

Among the things they use for medicine against anger are the corn kernels that are located at the beginning and root of the spike or ear. These kernels have their points contrary to their root—backwards and in the opposite direction to the rest on that particular ear. It is to this inverted position that the Indians attribute the contrary effect the incantation and spell have on affection and hatred. To the corn kernels they apply these words, which they believe give the kernels added strength and power and allow them to effect the change they seek. . . . After the conjured corn has been ground, it is administered orally, as either *atole* or chocolate, to the person whose will or affection they want to change.

Ruiz de Alarcón (IV:1)

Against Anger

Ruiz de Alarcón (IV:1)

tla xihualhuian	come forth
Tlazopilli	*Tlazopilli*
Centeotl	*Centeotl*
ticcehuiz	you will calm down
cozauhqui yollotli	the yellow heart
quizaz	the green anger
xoxouhqui tlahuelli	the yellow anger
cozauhqui tlahuelli	will come out
nicquixtiz	I shall make it leave
nictotocaz	I shall chase it away—
nitlamacazqui	I, Spirit in Flesh
niNahualteuctli	I, the Enchanter
niquitiz tlamazcazqui	through this drink
Pahtecatl	Medicine Spirit
Yollocuepcatzin	will change this heart

Home Spirit

you lock
windows
doors

but I'm
inside:
am you

To Cast Sleep

Ruiz de Alarcón (II:2)

nomatca nehuatl	I myself
niMoyohualitoatzin	I, the One-Called-Night
in ic nehuatl	because I am
in ic ChiucnauhTopan	from the Nine-*Topan*
in icuac . . .	at this time . . .
tla xihualhuian	come forth
in Temicxoch	Dream-Flower—
in cuac	at this time
in ic nicanato	I went to take
in nohueltiuh	my elder sister
ChiucnauhTopan	to the Nine-*Topan*
nitlamacazqui	I, Spirit in Flesh
in nohueltiuh	whose sister
Xochiquetzal	*Xochiquetzal*
in ic cenca quipiaya	was so guarded
in tlamacazque	by the priests
in mochintin in cuauhtin	by all the eagles
in ocelome	and the jaguars
in ayac huel calaquiya	no one could enter
in ic nictzatzili	shouting I called
in cochiztli	for sleep to come
in ic ChiucnauhMictlan	and they all went
yaque	to Nine-*Mictlan*
in ic nehuatl	since I am
niXolotl	the Double
niCapanilli	the Joint Cracker
in zan tlalhuiz	who mindlessly
nohuiyan nitzatzi	cries out everywhere

tla xihuallauh	come forth
tlamacazqui Ce-Tecpatl	spirit One Flint—
tla xoconmatiti	go and see
in nohueltiuh cuix ococh	if my elder sister's sleeping
ye nicquixtitiuh	I'm going to take her away
in ic ahmo nechelehuizque	and her brothers
yehuantin	won't harm me
ixquichtin ioquichtihuan	none of her men
ahmo nechelehuizque	will harm me
in ic ye nichuicaz	when I take her
in ChiucnauhMictlan	to Nine-Mictlan
in oncan nichuicaz	I will take her to
tlalli inepantla	the center of the earth
in ic oncan nicmacatiuh	I will deliver her to
in Moyohualitoatzin	the One-Called-Night
in ic nauhcan	from the four directions
niccuepaz	I will bring her back
in ic ahmo quimatiz	and she won't feel a thing
nehuatl	I am
niYaotl	the Warrior
niMoquequeloatzin	the Mocker—
in ic ye nicahahuiltiz	soon I shall give her pleasure
in ic ye niquincuepaz	soon I shall change the others
niquinmiccacuepaz	put them to sleep as dead
in niYaotl	I, the Warrior
niMoquequeloatzin	I, the Mocker—
in ic ye niquinmacaz	soon I shall do this to them
in ic yohuallahuanazque	and all shall be drunk with night

To Undo the Sleep Spell

Ruiz de Alarcón (II:2)

in ic niquimanatiuh	I'm going to take them back
tlalli inepantla	from the center of the Earth
in ic nauhcampa	from the four directions:
in ahmo nelli in	it's not true that
no niquincuepa	I changed them—
in ahmo cochiya	they were not sleeping
in ahmo oyaca	they did not go
ChiucnauhMictlan	to Nine-*Mictlan*
in ahmo nelli oquinhuicac	neither did the One-Called-Night
in Moyohualitoatzin	truly take them away
ea!	come on!
ye niquincuepa	I've already brought them back
in yehuatl in Temicxoch	from their Dream-Flower—
in nehuatl	I am
in niYohuallahuantzin	the Night-Drinker

89

For Finding Affection

Ruiz de Alarcón (IV:2)

Tezcatepec	on Mirror Mountain
nenamicoyan	the place of encounters
nicihuanotza	I call for a woman
nicihuacuica	I sing out for her
nonnentlamati	crying up
nihualnentlamati	crying down
ye noconhuica	already at my side
in nohueltiuth	my elder sister
in Xochiquetzal	Xochiquetzal
Ce-Coatl ica	with One Serpent
apantihuitz	as her mantle
Ce-Coatl ica	with One Serpent
cuitlalpitihuitz	as her belt
tzonilpitihuitz	as ribbon in her hair
ye yalhua	yesterday
ye huiptla	the day before
ica nichoca	I wept
ica ninentlamati	I cried
ca mach nelli teotl	she is a true goddess
ca mach nelli mahuiztic	she is a true power
cuix quin moztla	tomorrow?
cuix quin huiptla	the day after?
niman aman	right now!
nomatca nehuatl	I myself
niTelpochtli	I, the Youth
niYaotl	I, the Warrior:

no nitonac	I sunshine
no nitlathuic	I dawn
cuix zan cana onihualla	risen from nowhere?
cuix zan cana onihualquiz	born from nowhere?
ompa onihualla	I have risen, I was born
ompa onihualquiz . . .	of a woman's flower . . .

The words that belong here, even though somewhat disguised, are omitted out of concern for modest and chaste ears.

ca mach nelli teotl	she is a true goddess
ca mach nelli mahuiztic	she is a true power
cuix quin moztla	will I find her
cuix quin huiptla	tomorrow?
niquittaz	the day after?
niman aman	right now!
nomatca nehuatl	I myself
niTelpochtli	I, the Youth
niYaotl	I, the Warrior
cuix nelli niYaotl	am I truly war-like?
ahmo nelli niYaotl	I am not truly at war—
zan niCihuayotl	I'm of a woman's womb

For Love

enchanted
words
at dawn

a handful
of flowers
and stars

Nature

the nature
of poetry's
nature

the nature
of religion's
nature

the nature
of nature's
nature

For Bathing

Ruiz de Alarcón (IV:3)

tla xihualhuia	come forth
Ayahuitl Itzon	Mist Hair
Poctli Itzon	Smoke Hair
Nonan	Mother of mine
Chalchiuhcueye	*Chalchiuhcueye*
Iztac-Cihuatl	White Woman
tla xihualhuian	come forth
in anTlazolteteo	Goddesses of Filth:
in tiCuaton	you, *Cuaton*
in tiCaxxoch	you, *Caxxoch*
in tiTlahui	you, *Tlahui*
in tiXapel	you, *Xapel*
xinechitztimamaniqui	remove
yayauhqui tlazolli	the dark filth
iztac tlazolli	the white filth
xoxouhqui tlazolli	the green filth
onihualla	I have come
nitlamacazqui	I, Spirit in Flesh
niNahualteuctli	I, the Enchanter
Xoxouhqui Tlaloc	Green Tlaloc
Iztac Tlaloc	White Tlaloc:
ma noca	beware
tehuahti	of raising against me
ma noca	beware
timilacatzoti	of turning against me
nomatca nehuatl	I myself
nitlamacazqui	I, Spirit in Flesh
niNahualteuctli	I, the Enchanter

94

Seer

I sweep
and clean
my house

I burn
the trash
get rid
of obstacles

my house
now has
no walls
no anger
or sorrow

I am resting:
my *hamaca*
is a canoe
crossing
the Milky Way

Visions

at night
I see
by ear
by hand
by heart

Listen

every
landscape

a wondrous
story

Oracle

"it's me"
I say
"it's us"
rocks echo

5. Diviners

*. . . para adivinar por las manos no lo
hacen por las rayas, costumbre y
superstición de gitanos, sino midiendo
el medio brazo izquierdo desde el
codo a la punta de los dedos con la
mano derecha, tendiendo el palmo por
el medio brazo. . . .*

. . . in divining with the hands, the
Indians don't read palms—the
custom and superstition of the
Gypsies—but measure the left
forearm from the elbow to the
fingertips, stretching out the span of
the right hand on the forearm. . . .

Ruiz de Alarcón (V:1)

Divining with the Hands

Ruiz de Alarcón (V:1)

nomatca nehuatl	I myself
nitlamacazqui	I, Spirit in Flesh
ninahuealtecutli	I, the Enchanter
niXolotl	I, the Double
tla cuel he!	help now!
tla xihualhuian	come forth
tlamacazqui	spirit
Chiucnauhtlatecapanilli	Nine-Times-Crushed-One
Chiucnauhtlatlamatelolli	Nine-Times-Crumbled-One
Chiucnauhtlatezohtzontli	Nine-Times-Powdered-One
Xoxouhqui Tlamacazqui	Green Spirit
nonan	mother
nota	father of mine
Citlalcueye ipiltzin	son of the Milky Way
nonan Ce-Tochtli Aquetztimani	my mother One-Rabbit Supine
Tzotzotlacatoc	you who are resplendent
Tezcatl in zan hualpopocatimani	the Smoking Mirror of Earth
ayac tlatlacoz	no one shall fail
ayac huexcapehuaz	no one shall grumble
ca nictaennamiqui	now I kiss
Macuiltonale	the five solar spirits
ca oniquinhualhuicac	I've brought forth

Here the diviner puts his hands together, as if praying, crosses one thumb over the other, and kisses them.

tla xihualhuian	come on
noquichtihuan	elder brothers of mine
in Macuiltonaleque	five solar spirits each
cemithualeque	one-courtyard-owners
tzoneptzitzinme	pearly-headed ones

101

tla toconittacan	let us go and see
tonahualtezcauh	our enchanted mirror
ac teotl	who is the god
ac mahuiztli	who is the power
ic tlapoztequi	who is messing up
ic tlaxaxamania	who is shattering
ic quixpoloa	who is undoing
in tochalchiuh	our jade
in tocozqui	our jewel
in toquetzal?	our plume?
tla xihualhuian	come on
tla toconotlecahuican	let us climb up
tochalchiuhecahuaz	our jade ladder
toMictlanhecahuaz	our *Mictlan* ladder
ahmo quin moztla	not tomorrow
ahmo quin huiptla	or the day after
zan niman	but right now
axcan toconittazque	we shall see
ac ye quimictia	who is killing
in teteoh impiltzin	the son of the gods
nomatca nehuatl	I myself
nitlamacazqui	I, Spirit in Flesh
nitlamantini	I, the Sage
ninihmatcaticitl	I, the Healer
niMictlanTeuctli:	I, Lord of *Mictlan:*
quen ye quitlamachtia?	will this cure him?
cuix quitlanahuitiz?	will he get worse?
ca cuix achicatiz?	will he last some time?

102

Prayer to Fire

Ruiz de Alarcón (V:2)

tla xihualhuian	come forth
nota	father of mine
Nahui-Acatl Milintica	Four Reed Flaming
Tzoncoztli	Yellow Hair
TlahuizcalpanTeuctli	Lord of the House-of-Dawn
Teteo Inta	Father of the Gods
Teteo Innan	Mother of the Gods
ca oniquinhualhuicac	I've brought forth
nonanhualteohuan	my enchanted gods
noztacteohuan	my white gods
tla xihualhuian	come forth
Macuiltonaleque	five solar spirits each
tzoneptzitzinme	pearly-headed ones
in zan ce imithual	one-courtyard-owners
zan ce inchayahuacauh	brackets of a rail
tla toconittacan	let us look at
tonalhualtezcauh, etc.	our enchanted mirror, etc.
ca niman	right now
aman	it shall be
nomatca nehuatl	I myself
nOxomoco	I, *Oxomoco*
niCipactonal	I, *Cipactonal*
nicmati Huehueh	I, the Old Man's friend
nicmati Ilama	I, the Old Woman's friend
niMictlanmati	I, *Mictlan* traveler
niTopanmati	I, *Topan* traveler
nomatca nehuatl	I myself
nitlamacazqui	I, Spirit in Flesh
niNahualteuctli	I, the Enchanter

Tobacco

piciete:
sacred dust

with lime:
tenexiete

key
medicine

as smoke:
praising mist

messenger
to heavens

puffs
blessing

the lips
the hands

the living
quarters

El tal sortílego escoge de una
mazorca y de entre mucho maíz los
granos más asomados y hermosos,
de los cuales entresaca tal vez
diez y nueve granos y tal vez veinte
y cinco granos, y esta diferencia
causa la que tienen en ponerlos
sobre el lienzo en que se echa
la suerte; escogidos los dichos
granos el tal sortílego, les corta los
picos con los dientes, luego tiende
delante de sí un lienzo doblado y
bien extendido de manera que
no haga arruga, luego pone sobre
él una parte de los granos según la
cantidad que cogió.

El que escogió diez y nueve
pone al lado derecho cuatro granos
muy parejos, la haz hacia arriba
y las puntas hacia el lado
izquierdo, pone otros tantos con el
mismo orden y luego arroja otros
cuatro sin orden enfrente de sí y
queda con siete granos en la mano;
otros ponen cuatro en cada esquina
y quedan con nueve en la mano,
que todos hacen veinte y cinco;
otros ponen en cada esquina siete y
arrojan dos enfrente sin orden y
quedan con

From his chosen ear of corn, the
fortune teller selects nineteen
or twenty-five of the most out-
standing and beautiful kernels,
depending on his particular
method of divination. Then he
bites off their nibs with his teeth
and places them before him on
a cloth that has been stretched
and smoothed so it contains no
wrinkles.

The one who has chosen
nineteen puts four very similar
kernels on the right side, with
points facing and an equal
number on the left side, with
points facing right. Then he
randomly flings another four in
front of him while holding the
remaining seven in his hand.
Those who use twenty-five
kernels put four in each corner
and keep nine in the hand.
Others put seven in each corner,
toss two in front, and keep nine
in the hand, making thirty-
nine in all. . . .

Finally the seer pronounces
the words of this spell while
tossing the kernels in his hand

nueve en la mano, que todos hacen
treinta y nueve. . . .

  Dematando las palabras del
conjuro, arroja el maíz que tenía
en la mano en medio del lienzo,
y según caen los maíces juzga la
suerte. La regla que de ordinario
tienen en juzgarla, es que si los
maíces caen la faz hacia arriba, es
buena suerte, v. gr. será buena la
medicina sobre que se consulta,
o parecerá la persona o cosa
perdida que se busca, y al contrario
si los maíces caen la faz hacia
abajo. . . .

onto the middle of the cloth, and
he determines the fortune
according to how they fall. The
usual rule is that if the kernels
fall face up, the fortune is good—
for example, the medicine upon
which one has made consultation
will be good, or the person or
thing one seeks will show up. The
contrary is true if the kernels fall
face down. . . .

Ruiz de Alarcón (V:3)

106

Divining with Corn

Ruiz de Alarcón (V:3)

tla xihualmohuica	welcome
Tlazopilli	*Tlazopilli*
Chicome-Coatl	Seven Snake
tla xihualhuian	come forth
Macuiltonaleque	five solar spirits each
cemithualeque	one-courtyard-owners
aman yequen eh	now at last
tla tiquittati	let us go see
in incamanal	their joke
in inetequipachol	his worry
cuix quin moztla?	will it be tomorrow?
cuix quin huiptla?	the day after?
ca iman	right now
aman	it shall be
nomatca nehuatl	I myself
niCipactonal	I, *Cipactonal*
niHuehueh	I, the Ancient One
ye itic nontlachiaz	soon I shall see
in namox	in my book
in notezcauh	in my mirror
in tla quinamiqui pahtzintli	if this medicine cures him
ahnozo motlanahuitia	or if he gets worse

Tonal

if you lose
your *tonal*

might as well
be dead

Divining by Looking in the Water

Ruiz de Alarcón (VI:2)

The diviners who can read fate by looking in the water, *Atlan Tlachixque,* begin with the following incantation. When they hold the child over the water, if they see that the child's face is dark, as if covered by a shadow, they judge his future to be absent of fate and fortune. If the child's face appears bright in the water, they say he is not sick, or that the indisposition is very slight. In this case, they conclude he will get well without a cure, or they administer a treatment of incense. . . .

tla cuel!	come now!
tla xihuallauh	come forth
nonan	Mother
Chalchiuhcueye	*Chalchiuhcueye*
Chalchihuitl Icue	Jade-Skirted-One
Chalchihuitl Ihuipil	Jade-Bloused-One
Xoxouhqui Icue	Green-Skirted-One
Xoxouhqui Ihuipil	Green-Bloused-One
Iztac-Cihuatl	White Woman
tla toconittilican	let us look at
in icnopiltzintli	this poor little child
azo oquicauh	perhaps his *tonal*
itonaltzin	has left him

Wiser

now I know
why my father

would go out
and cry

in the rain

Yoliliztli / Life in Motion

something
more than nothing
like morning
sunlight or air

something
around a kiss
something
within a flower

something light
something sweet
something deep
something free

something else
capable of turning
caterpillars into
butterflies

Messengers

to Victor di Suvero

chairs
doors
walls

lay
themselves
messages

down
above
everywhere

murmurs
secrets
bits of

dreams
to each
other

Flowers

a day
is all
we last
a breath!

We're One

sea
dust
tear
pollen

6. Healers

Father
look, I have your pure cane
your fresh cane, you
my patron Mother
look how poor I am
how humble I am
poor woman am I
humble woman am I
tender woman, abundant woman am I
woman of big roots am I,
woman rooted below the water am I
woman who sprouts am I
woman like a begonia am I
I am going to the sky,
in your sight, before your glory
there my paper, my Book remains
woman who stops the world am I
legendary woman healer am I
my feelings are satisfied
my heart is satisfied
because I carry your heart, I
because I carry your heart, Christ
because I carry your heart, Father

María Sabina
(from a shamanic ceremony
on the night of July 12,
1958, in Huatla de Jiménez,
Oaxaca, Mexico)

Birth

Cuaton
Caxxoch
Goddesses
of Love

burst
the dam
of life

let the five
solar spirits
in each hand
become a net

and catch
this child
of the gods

Reconciling

to Lupe Macías

Chalchiuhcueye
Mother Water
lakes, stars
snakes and all:

everyone is your *cuate*
a mirror to yourself:
break up the illusion
take off the mask

you are naked
you are stripped
you are bone
you are dust

don't look back
look within:
accept the woman
the spirit is female

read the silence
enter the silence
smell the fire
of each morning

honor the dirt
in your fingernails
restore the balance
of your Mother

water of one ocean
flower of the Sun
walking calendar:
don't shame yourself!

In Ixtli In Yollotl / Face and Heart

To J. P.

may our ears
hear
what nobody
wants to hear

may our eyes
see
what everyone
wants to hide

may our mouths
speak
our true faces
and hearts

may our arms
be branches
that give shade
and joy

let us be a drizzle
a sudden storm
let us get wet
in the rain

let us be the key
the hand the door
the kick the ball
the road

let us arrive
as children
to this huge
playground:

the universe

En esto le hice poner en buen recaudo, y antes de pasar un día de su prisión se juntó gran número de indios, que trayéndome un presente, me pidieron muy encarecidamente le soltase, porque era su remedio y consuelo y de todas sus enfermedades . . .

I had [Domingo Hernández] placed under good custody. Before he had spent a day in prison, a great number of Indians gathered. They brought me presents and begged very earnestly that I set him free because he was the remedy and consolation for all their illnesses . . .

Ruiz de Alarcón (VI:19)

Domingo Hernández

please
let him free
he's kind
our remedy

he's crossed
the Nine Rooms
he cures
    he heals

with *atlinan*
    water mother
with *yauhtli*
    sweet marigolds

let him
finish his wind:
"in Xoxohuix Tlamacazqui
    in Yayahuic Tlamacazqui
(Green Spirit
    Dark Spirit)
in Nomine Patris
    et Filii
        et Spiritus Sancti"

Herbs

in the market
herbs begin
to sing

a song
of small leaves
of green thumbs

ground herbs
water herbs
sky herbs

herbs for
all pains
and afflictions

the root
of *coanenepilli*
for sunstroke

drops
of *tenexiete*
for earaches

for swollen heads
the root
of *chalalatli*

mezquite sap
for curing
the eyes

toothaches gone
with *copal*
and *piciete*

teas
    oils
        incenses

sore throats
chest pains
bye bye

I put
my wet feet
on heated stones

and start
walking
barefoot

over and over
my own
back bones

For Strained Chests

Ruiz de Alarcón (VI:14)

This affliction comes from working too much with the arms, and is frequently seen in those who dig in the mines. To remedy a strained chest, *piciete* (crushed tobacco) and *yauhtli* (anise) are applied along with this spell:

tla xihuallauh	come
Chiucnauhtlatetzotzon	Nine-Times-Powdered-One
Chiucnauhtlatecapani	Nine-Times-Crushed-One
yayauhqui coacihuiztli	dark pain
xoxouhqui coacihuiztli	green pain:
ac tlacatl	who is the person
ac mahuiztli	who is the power
in ye quixpoloa	who is hurting
nomacehual	my fellow human?
tla xictotoca	chase it away
tla xihuian	go to it
tlazotli	precious ones
campa in omotecato	where does it lie?
[Nahuatl text is missing here]	in my enchanted rib cage?
	in my enchanted backbone?
itic in nonahualtzontecomatl	to my enchanted head
tictocaticalaquiz	go swiftly
tlamacazque	you, spirits
Macuiltonaleque	five solar spirits each
ma ammopinauhtitin	do your duty
Cozauhqui-Cihuatl	you, Yellow Woman

124

Tonantzin

Madre	Mother
¿aquí estás	are you here
con nosotros?	with us?
enjuáganos	wipe up
el sudor	our sweat
las lágrimas	our tears
Coatlicue	*Coatlicue*
tú que reinas	you who rule
sobre las serpientes	over snakes
Chalchiuhcueye	*Chalchiuhcueye*
haznos	grant us
el favor	our request
Citlalcueye	*Citlalcueye*
que nos guíen	let your stars
tus estrellas	guide us
Guadalupe	*Guadalupe*
sé nuestra aurora	be our dawn
nuestra esperanza	our hope
¡bandera	the flag
y fuego de	and fire of
nuestra rebelión!	our rebellion!

Cihuacoatl

in the barrios
La Llorona
has run out
of tears

For Bone Fractures

Ruiz de Alarcón (VI:22)

tle oax nohuetiuh	what have my elder sisters—
in Chicuetecpacihuatl	Eight Flint Woman and
Tlaloccihuatl	*Tlaloc* Woman—done?
omonapaloque	they've embraced
omomacochoque	they've reduced
teteo impiltzin	the child of the gods
ca nehuatl	but I am
nitlamacazqui	the Spirit in Flesh
niQuetzalcóatl	*Quetzalcóatl*
niyani Mictlan	I've gone to *Mictlan*
niyani Topan	I've gone to *Topan*
niyani ChiucnauhMictlan	I've gone to Nine-*Mictlan*
ompa niccuiz	there I will get
in Mictlanomitl	the *Mictlan* bone
otlatlacoque	they've messed up—
in tlamacazque	the spirits
in teuhtotome	the dust-birds
otlaxaxamanique	something they shattered
otlapoztecque	something they broke
auh in axcan	but now we shall glue it
ticzazalozque	back together
ticpatizque	we shall heal it
tla cuel	come now
nomazacoamecatzin	my deersnake rope
tla nican xontlapixto	go stand watch here
ma nen tontlatlaco	beware of messing up—
mopan necoz in moztla	I'll see you tomorrow

Massage

hands put
our pains
to sleep

lead them
as fish to
whirlpools

Acupuncture for the Back

Ruiz de Alarcón (VI:23)

tla cuel!	come now!
xoxohuic coatl	green snake
cozahuic coatl	yellow snake
tlatlahuic coatl	red snake
iztac coatl	white snake
ye huitz	soon will come
iztac cuautlatzotzopitzqui	the white eagle puncturer
nohuiyan nemiz	she will be everywhere—
in tetl itic	inside the rocks
in cuahuitli itic	inside the trees
auh in ac in ipan aciz	whatever she finds
quicuaz	she will eat
quipopoloz	she will destroy

129

For Fevers

Ruiz de Alarcón (VI:29)

For fevers the Indians use remedies of *ololiuhqui, peyote, atlinan* ("water mother") or other herbs. The method is to grind the herb, dissolve it in cold water, then administer it as an enema with the following spell and incantation:

tla cuel!	come on!
tla xihuallauh	come now
Xoxouhqui-Cihuatl	Green Woman
tla xicpehuiti	take away
xoxouhqui totonqui	the green heat
yayauhqui totonqui	the dark heat
tlatlauhqui totonqui	the red heat
cozauhqui totonqui	the yellow heat
ye onca nimitztitlan	now I send you there
Chicomoztoc	to the Seven Caves
ahmo quin moztla	not tomorrow
ahmo quin huiptla	or the day after
niman axcan	but right now
ticquixtiz	you shall banish this
ac teotl	who is the god
ac mahuiztli	who is the power
in ye quixpoloa	who is destroying
motlachihualtzin	your creation?
nomatca nehuatl	I myself
niNahualteuctli	I, the Enchanter

For Fatigue and Body Pains

Ruiz de Alarcón (VI:31)

For fatigue, which the Indians call *cuacuauhtiliztli* ("stiffness"), and for body pains, the method of treatment is to cause an evacuation by administering an enema or clyster. The one who practices this cure heats the soles of the feet and the heels, something which they call *ytetleiza* ("fire-treading"), and massages the body from the kidneys and loins to the ankles while adding this spell:

tla xihuallauh	come here
cozahuic neahanalli	yellow relaxer
xoxouhqui neahanalli	green relaxer:
nican tictemozque	here we shall seek out
in cozauhqui cuacuauhtiliztli	the yellow stiffness
xoxouhqui cuacuauhtiliztli	the green stiffness

Magadalena Petronila Xochiquetzal, an old blind woman from Huitzoco, used to practice this fraud. Another woman called Justina, from the same village, used to employ the herb that they call *tzopilotl,* also applied as an enema, with this next spell:

tla xihuallauh	come here
Iztac-Cihuatl	White Woman:
tla xocompopoloti	go and destroy
in xoxouhqui coacihuiztli	the green pain
yayahuic coacihuiztli	the dark pain
(quitoznequi cuacuauhtiliztli)	(meaning the stiffness)

NOTE

At this point, it seems to me that I should speak of something that should be of interest to any person whose charge is the governance and customs of these natives, something so rooted and accepted among them, and so harmful that the Enemy (who is vigilant for our detriment) has introduced, taking advantage of their natural weakness and inclination.

This is, that at the same time that they are compelled to personal service, in farm work as well as in the mines, where they usually experience so much damage to their bodily health from excessive work—labor which borne out of love for God would be of much spiritual benefit—but the Devil has established his league against it by persuading them that, if they get drunk to excess before going to work, they will gather such strength and vigor that they would easily be able to bear such tasks, and following that, to recover their strength lost in drunkenness. They call these harmful drunken sprees *necehualiztli* ("refreshing oneself").

Thus, with their drinking and the intolerable work that they have, they end up getting sick and dying, without taking warning from the continual deaths that come about each day from these drunken sprees. For this reason, the ministers and curates ought to try to convince them of the serious harm that comes to their bodies and souls from this. The same goes for the secular authorities: *in virga ferrea* ("with a rod of iron"), since experience shows that no gentle means is of use in extirpating this infernal vice, at the hands of which such a great multitude is dying. This miserable generation is entirely destroying and consuming itself, taking death in their hands.

Holocaust

your eyes
don't see

your ears
are plugged

this hell's
your invention

we're morning
flowers cut

bleeding in
your altar

vases
fields mines

Working Hands

we clean
your room

we do
your dishes

a footnote
for you

but hands
like these

one day
will write

the main text
of this land

Not Poems

just ink
on paper
like air
like you

The Story of *Yappan*

Ruiz de Alarcón (VI:32)

In the first era, when those that now are animals were humans, there was one whose name was *Yappan*. For the sake of improving his condition in the transmutation that he felt near, in order to placate the gods and capture their benevolence, he went off alone to do penance in abstinence and chastity. He lived on a rock called *Tehuehuetl* ("Stone-Drum"). Because *Yappan* persevered in his intentions they placed someone called *Yaotl* ("the Warrior") to watch him.

During this time, *Yappan* was tempted by some women but not overcome. Meanwhile the two sister goddesses, *Citlalcueye* and *Chalchiuhcueye* (who are the Milky Way and the Water), foresaw that *Yappan* was going to be turned into a scorpion and that, if he persisted in his purpose, after being converted into a scorpion, he would kill all those he stung. Seeking a remedy for this bad scenario, they decided that their sister, the goddess *Xochiquetzal,* should go down to tempt *Yappan*. She descended to where *Yappan* was and said to him:

Xochiquetzal:

"noquichtiuh
Yappan
onihualla
nimohueltiuh
niXochiquetzal
nimitztlapaloco
nimitzciauhquetzaco"

Xochiquetzal:

"dear brother
Yappan
I am here
I, your elder sister
Xochiquetzal
have come to greet you
I've come to meet you"

Yappan:

"otihuallauh
nohueltiuhe
Xochiquetzal"

Yappan:

"welcome
dear sister
Xochiquetzal"

Xochiquetzal:

"onihualla
campa ye nitlecoz"

Xochiquetzal:

"I am down here
where can I climb up?"

Yappan:

　"xicchie
　ye ompa niyauh"

Yappan:

　"wait
　I'm going down for you"

At that, the goddess *Xochiquetzal* climbed up and, covering him with
her *huipil* ("blouse"), he failed in his purpose (of chastity). The
cause of this fall was that *Xochiquetzal* was a stranger and a goddess
who came from the heavens, which they call *chicnauhtopan,* which
means "from the nine places." With this, the spy, *Yaotl,* who had not
fallen asleep, said to *Yappan:*

Yaotl:

　"*ahmo tipinahua
　tlamacazqui Yappan
　otitlatlaco*

　"*in quexquich cahuitl
　tlimonemitiz in tlalticpac*

　"*ahmo tle huel in tlaltipac
　ahmo tle huel tictequipanoz*

　"*mitztocayotizque
　in macehualtin 'tiColotl'*

　"*ca nican nimitztocayotia
　nimitzticamati 'tiColotl'*

　"*xihualhuian
　iuhque tiyez*"

Yaotl:

　"aren't you ashamed
　priest *Yappan*
　of messing up?

　"however long
　you live on earth

　"you shall do nothing well
　you shall achieve nothing

　"common folks
　will call you 'Scorpion'

　"for here I call you
　I name you 'Scorpion'

　"come forth
　for you shall be this way"

137

Narrator:

"oquiquechcoton
oquiquechpanoh
itzontecon

"yehuatl ica itoca
'Tzonteconmama'"

Narrator:

"he beheaded him
he carried on his shoulders
his head

"because of this he is called
'Head-Carrier'"

After being beheaded, Yappan was immediately transformed into a scorpion, and Yaotl went after Yappan's wife, cut off her head and transformed her into a scorpion. She was called Tlahuitzin ("Red-Ochre"). And since Yappan had sinned, the goddess Citlalcueye decided that not all those who were stung by a scorpion would die. And Yaotl was changed into a locust, which they call Ahuaca Chapullin ("Avocado Locust") or Tzonteconmamama ("Heads-Carrier").

Against Scorpion's Sting and Poison

Ruiz de Alarcón (VI:32)

nomatca nehuatl	I myself
niTlamacazqui	I, priest
Chicome-Xochitl	Seven Flower:
tla xihualhuian	come forth
Tlamacazqui Yappan	priest *Yappan*
Huitzcol	Curved Thorn
tle ica in teca timocacayahua?	why do you mock people?
cuix ahmo ye ticmati	don't you know by now
ahmo ye moyollo quimati	don't you know in your heart
in omitznezahualpoztequito	she went to break your fast
nohueltiuh	—my elder sister
Xochiquetzal	Xochiquetzal—
in ompa Tehuehueticpac	there on top of Stone Drum
in ompa in ica	there where you
otimocacayauh?	mocked her?
ahmo tle in huel ticchihuaz	there's nothing you can do
ahmo tle in huel tictequipanoz	there's nothing you can cause
nepa hueca	make fun of people
teca ximocacayahuati	far away from here
nepa hueca	amuse yourself with people
teca ximahuiltiti	far away from here
tla xihualhuia	come forth
nonan Tlalteuctli	*Tlalteuctli*, Mother Earth
zan ihuiyan xictlacahuati	calm down quietly
in Tlamacazqui Yappan	the priest *Yappan*
Pelxayaque	the Bare Mask

| ma zan ihuiyan quiza | let him leave quietly |
| ma zan ihuiyan mitztlacahui | let him depart unnoticed |

| cuix quin moztla | will he go tomorrow |
| cuix quin huiptla yaz? | or the day after? |

| ca niman | right now |
| aman | it shall be |

in tlacamo quizaz	if he doesn't leave
in tlacamo yaz	if he doesn't go
ca oc nehuatl nicmati	I will know
in tleh ipan nicchihuaz	what to do about it!

If the venom has already taken possession of the patient, the conjurer invokes *Xochiquetzal* by saying:

| noquichtiuh Pelxayaque | brother Bare Mask |
| ahmo tipinahua? | aren't you ashamed? |

| tleh ica in teca timocacayahua? | why do you make fun of people? |

| tle ica in teca timahuiltia? | why do you amuse yourself with people? |

cuix ahmo ye ticmati	don't you know by now
ahmo quimattica in moyollo	don't you know in your heart
in onimitznezahualpoztequito	I went to break your fast
in ompa Tehuehueticpac	there on top of Stone Drum
in niXochiquetzal	I, *Xochiquetzal*—
in ompa nohuan oticoch	there where you slept with me?

onihualla	I am here
in nimohueltituh	I, your elder sister
niXochiquetzal	I, *Xochiquetzal*
nimitzlapaloco	I've come to greet you
mimitzciauhquetzaco	I've come to meet you
za ihuiyan xictlalcahui	just leave alone
in nomacehual	my fellow human
tla nimitzhuipiltepoya	let me protect you with my *huipil*
tla nimitzhuipillapacho	let me cover you with my *huipil*
tla nimitzhuipilquimilo	let me wrap you with my *huipil*
za ihuiyan xicochi	just sleep quietly
tla nimitzmacochihui	let me embrace you
tla nimitznapalo	let me take you in my arms
tla nimitznahuatequi	let me kiss you

If the conjurer is a man, he covers the sick person with a blanket, embracing and caressing him. If the healer is a woman, she does likewise with her *huipil,* and also takes a ribbon or small cord from her hair and ties off the wounded limb of the sick person, saying:

noquichtiuh	elder brother
ahmo tipanahua	aren't you ashamed
titeelehuia?	of hurting people?

iuhqui tiyez in	you shall be like this . . .

[Here the conjurer draws a symbol which Ruiz de Alarcón had painted in the margin of his original text; this symbol is unfortunately now missing in the extant copy of the *Tratado*.]

iuhqui tiyez in	you shall be like this . . .

[missing symbol is repeated]

nican nimitzilpico	here I've come to tie you up
nimitztzacuilico	I've come to stop you

zan nican	right here
tlantica in monemac	your power ends
ahmo tipanoz	you shall not pass!

NEW DAY

. . . El chasquido del rayo
abría zanjas de luz
en tus ojos negros y
en la noche
del agua

Y en mí nacía la tormenta

. . . Thunder
opened chasms of light
in your dark eyes
in the night
on the water

And in me the storm was born

Lucha Corpi

Tepeyollotli

water's
the heart of
the mountain

its voice:
a jaguar
of echoes

New Day

from the hilltop
near my village
in the distance
by the cornfields

I saw their glitter
their luster
are those giant deer?
are they laughing?

and I heard
listened to
the soulbirds:
"trees are crying"

a thorn
pierced my tongue
and I prayed
bleeding

untied my long
black hair
threw to the sky
my father's bundle

soon night turned
me into a shadow
big enough to cover
the whole valley

enter and fuel
their own campfires
awaiting
for the new day!

Moon

celestial
drop of milk
of our Mother's
breast

Sun's Children

although
we may lose
in battle

we will win
this war
in peace

Night

how vast
how enormous
how great
this empire
of darkness

and yet
disarmed
by one
needle
of light

In Xochitl In Cuicatl

cada árbol	every tree
un hermano	a brother
cada monte	every hill
una pirámide	a pyramid
un oratorio	a holy spot
cada valle	every valley
un poema	a poem
in xochitl	*in xochitl*
in cuicatl	*in cuicatl*
flor y canto	flower and song
cada nube	every cloud
una plegaria	a prayer
cada gota	every rain
de lluvia	drop
un milagro	a miracle
cada cuerpo	every body
una orilla	a seashore
al mar	a memory
un olvido	at once lost
encontrado	and found
todos juntos:	we all together:
luciérnagas	fireflies
de la noche	in the night
soñando	dreaming up
el cosmos	the cosmos

150

Glossary

All words derived from Nahuatl if not otherwise noted

Acaxochtzin. (Reed-Flower), from *acatl,* "reed," *xochitl,* "flower," and the honorific suffix *-tzin;* it is a ritual name for the deer.

Aguamiel. The liquid drawn from the core of the maguey plant before it is fermented and turned into *pulque;* in Spanish it literally means "honey water."

Antiguos. Spanish for "ancient ones."

Atlinan. (Water-Mother), medicinal herb; from *atl,* "water," and *inan,* "it is its mother."

Atole. A thick drink or gruel made of corn meal of various consistencies and flavors; derived from *atolli,* which is formed by *atl,* "water," and *tlaolli,* "corn."

Aztec. Nahuatl-speaking group that migrated south from *Aztlán,* "Place of herons," which many contemporary Chicanos identify as their U.S. Southwest homeland and which is the origin of the word *Aztec;* they were also known as the *Mexica* (pronounced "Meshica"), from which *Mexicano* and *Chicano* are derived. In 1325 the Aztecs founded *Tenochtitlan* on a small island in Lake Texcoco where an eagle was devouring a serpent; they aggressively conquered the surrounding Indian groups and were themselves vanquished by new diseases and a combined Indian-Spanish army led by Hernán Cortés in 1521.

Camotes. Sweet potatoes, from *camotli.*

Capanilli. (Joint-Cracker), in the *Tratado,* the name occurs only in apposition to *Xolotl.*

Caxxoch. (Bowl-Flower), from *caxxochitl,* from *caxitl,* "bowl," and *xochitl,* "flower"; one of the four *Tlazolteteo,* Goddesses of Love and Filth.

Centeotl. (Ear-of-Corn God), from *centli,* "dried ear of corn," and *teotl,* "god"; Ruiz de Alarcón translated it as "the only god," a misinterpretation since he takes here *cen-* to mean "one."

Cenzontle. Derived by apocope from *centzontlatolltototl,* "bird of four hundred songs or voices"; from *centzontli,* "four hundred," *tlatolli,* "word," and *tototl,* "bird"; a tropical songbird appreciated for its great singing versatility.

Chalalatli. A tree with oblong leaves whose root is used to cure the swelling of the head.

Chalchiuhcueye. (Jade-Skirt-Owner), from *chalchihuitl,* "jade," *cueitl,* "skirt," and *ye,* "who owns"; Goddess of the Water.

Chichimec. Term for the nomadic and hunting Indian tribes arriving to Mesoamerica after the Toltecs in the 12th century; name of the barbaric tribes from the north; some have identified this word to mean "Dog-People." In the *Tratado,* it is also used as a metaphor for a fishhook.

Chicome-Coatl. (Seven Snake), from *chicome,* "seven" (*chic-ome,* "five-plus-two"), and *coatl,* "snake"; a calendaric name and Goddess of Corn; in the *Tratado,* it is used as a magical name for corn; it refers to a specific date marking the planting cycle of corn that some have identified as the March 21 Spring equinox.

Chicome-Xochitl. (Seven Flower), from *chicome,* "seven" (*chic-ome,* "five-plus-two"), and *xochitl,* "flower"; a calendaric name; it is a ritual name for the male deer.

Chicomoztoc. (Seven-Caves-Place), from *chicome,* "seven" (*chic-ome,* "five-plus-two"), *oztotl,* "cave," and the stem *-c,* meaning place; this name designates the mythical seven caves from which the Aztecs originated; in the *Tratado,* it is used as a metaphor for cavities.

Chiucnauhtlatecapanilli. (Nine-Times-Crushed-One), a metaphorical name for tobacco.

Chiucnauhtlatezohtzontli. (Nine-Times-Powdered-One), a metaphorical name for tobacco.

Chiucnauhtlatlamatelolli. (Nine-Times-Crumbled-One), a metaphorical name for tobacco.

Cihuacoatl. (Woman-Snake), from *cihuatl,* "woman," and *coatl,* "snake"; known as *La Llorona* in Mexico and the Southwest.

Cipactonal. (Alligator-Spirit), from *cipactli,* "alligator," and *tonal,* "spirit"; *cipactli* is also the glyph of the first day in the Mesoamerican 20-day month, symbolizing the first animal able to move from the sea to dry land; first woman in the Mesoamerican primordial couple; in Nahuatl mythology, she is credited (together with her spouse, *Oxomoco*) with originating the divinatory arts.

Citlalcueye. (Star-Skirt-Owner), from *citlalin,* "star," *cueitl,* "skirt," and *ye,* "who owns"; Nahuatl name for the Milky Way.

Coanenepilli. (Snake-Tongue), from *coatl,* "snake," and *nenepilli,* "tongue"; medicinal herb against snake bites, among other remedies.

Coatlicue. (Snake-Skirted-One), from *coatl,* "snake," and *icue,* "it is her skirt"; Fertility Goddess.

Codex Borbonicus. Book of Indian pictures and glyphs, probably completed before the arrival of the Europeans in the 16th century; original codex is found in the Palais Bourbon, Paris, France.

Codex Borgia. Book of Indian pictures and glyphs; original codex is found in the Vatican Library in Rome.

Codex Magliabechiano. Book of Indian pictures and glyphs; the original manuscript is now located in the Biblioteca Nazionale Centrale of Florence; it was once part of the personal library of Antonio da Marco Magliabechi, a Florentine bibliographer and man of letters of the late 17th century.

Copal. Tree resin used as incense; *copalli,* "incense."

Corazón. Spanish for "heart."

Cozauhqui. (Yellow), this color is usually associated with the east; *cozahuic* is another variant of *cozauhqui.*

Cuate. Term derived from Nahuatl, of common usage in Mexican/Chicano Spanish, meaning "twin," figuratively used for "close, intimate friends"; from *coatl,* "snake"; two snakes of fire form the exterior ring of the Aztec calendar stone marking the time when *Quetzalcoatl* meets his double, *Xolotl.*

Cuaton. (Small-Head), from *cuaitl,* "head," and the diminutive suffix, *-ton;* one of the four *Tlazolteteo,* Goddesses of Love and Filth.

Curandera. Spanish for "healer."

Flor. Spanish for "flower."

Guadalupe. Patron saint of Mexico, a syncretic religious figure that includes Mesoamerican, Christian, and Arabic elements; according to tradition she appeared and spoke in Nahuatl to Indian Juan Diego in Tepeyac where *Tonantzin,* "Our Mother Goddess," was worshipped; she has been espoused to several social movements and causes both in Mexico and the Southwest; for example, she was on the first Mexican flag of Father Miguel Hidalgo's Indian army fighting for independence from Spain in 1810, the banner of the Mestizo popular armies of Emiliano Zapata in the Mexican Revolution of 1910, and also appeared in California along picket signs in the 1965 Delano grape strike organized by Chicano union leader César Chávez.

Hamaca. Spanish word derived from a Taíno term; "hammock."

Huauhtli. Amaranth; cereal used in molding figurines which were then offered and shared as a ritual communion of thanksgiving after the first crop of the year.

Huehueh. (Old Man), a metaphor for fire; it is also another name for *Oxomoco;* in classical times, *Huehueteotl,* from *huehuetl,* "old man," and *teotl,* "god," was the name of the God of Fire, one of the oldest deities in Mesoamerica.

Huipil. A sleeveless cotton tunic used by Indian women as a blouse or dress.

Icnopiltzintli. (Orphan-Child), from *icnotl,* "orphan," and *piltzintli,* "child"; this is another name for *Centeotl,* but it may also be a common noun for "poor orphan."

In ixtli in yollotl. (Face and Heart), figurative phrase for truth and sincerity, formed by setting together *ixtli,* "face," and *yollotl,* "heart."

In xochitl in cuicatl. (Flower and Song), figurative phrase for poetry, formed by setting together *xochitl,* "flower," and *cuicatl,* "song"; Chicanos have used the Spanish equivalent, *floricanto,* to name the poetry and cultural festivals in their communities since the late 1960s.

Iztac. (White), this color is usually associated with the south.

La Llorona. Spanish for "Crying Woman," a mythical woman who cries up and down looking for her lost children around water sources, very much alive in folk legends throughout Mexico and the Southwest; derived from the Aztec legend of *Cihuacoatl,* Woman-Snake.

Maguey. Taíno term from the Caribbean region for the plant from which *aguamiel* (Spanish for "honey water") is drawn and turned into *pulque,* an alcoholic beverage when fermented; its Nahuatl name is *metl.*

Maíz. Spanish word derived from the Taíno name for corn; the Nahuatl equivalent is *tlaolli,* "dried, shelled corn," or *centli,* "dried, unshelled corn."

Matl. (The Hand), in the *Tratado* it is used as another name for *Quetzalcóatl.*

Mestizo. Spanish word that identifies a person of mixed racial/ethnic background; it does not have the negative connotations of its English equivalents, "half-breed," "half-caste"; it has been increasingly accepted as a self-identity term by Latinos both in Latin America and in the U.S.

Mezquite. A common spiny shrub or small tree in Mexico and the Southwest that produces a medicinal resin; from *mizquitli,* "tree of resin."

Mixcoacihuatl. (*Mixcoatl's* Woman), from *Mixcoatl,* "Cloud-Snake," and *cihuatl,* "woman"; it is the female deer.

Mixcoatl. (Cloud-Snake), from *mixtli,* "cloud," and *coatl,* "snake"; in classical times, *Mixcoatl* was the God of the Hunt.

Mictlan. (Land of the Dead), the underworld which consisted of nine levels, *ChiucnauhMictlan* (from *chiuc-nahui,* "five-plus-four"); by extension, it refers to the supernatural world as a whole.

Moquequeloatzin. (The-One-Who-Makes-Fun-of-Himself), another name for *Tezcatlipoca.*

Moyohualitoatzin. (One-Called-Night), in classical times, this was another manifestation of *Xipe ToTec,* a Fertility God.

Nahual. Derived from *nahualli,* "sorcerer," "magician"; in the *Tratado,* it signifies a sorcerer who supposedly is able to transform himself/herself into an animal or the animal that is the alter ego, *tonal,* or the guardian spirit that accompanies a person throughout his/her life.

Nahualteuctli. (The Enchanter), from *nahualli,* "sorcerer," and *teuctli,* "lord."

Nahuatl. Language from the Uto-Aztec linguistic family, which extended from the U.S. Southwest and Mexico to Central America; spoken by the Toltecs, Aztecs, Pipiles, and many other Indian groups; hundreds of Spanish and English words derive from Nahuatl; the term comes from the verb *nahuati,* "to speak clearly."

Nana. Familiar term for mother; from the endearment *nanatzin,* "little mother."

Nanahuatzin. (The Sun), the honorific name of *Nanahuahuatl,* "Pustulous-One"; Ruiz de Alarcón retells the myth of the creation of the sun in which a sick man afflicted with pustules and sores was the first to throw himself into a fire; flames cleansed him of all disease, and he came out beautiful and shining, converted into the sun.

Nomatca nehuatl. (I myself), magical formula for personal empowerment found in most Nahuatl spells in the *Tratado;* Ruiz de Alarcón translates it as a phrase, "I myself in person" or "I in person"; J.

Richard Andrews and Ross Hassig translate it as a sentence with *nehuatl* meaning "I am the one," or "it is I," and *nomatca* as an adverbial modifier, "in person."

Olchipinque. (Ones-Dripping-With-Rubber), in the *Tratado*, a metaphor for birds.

Ollin. (Movement), the Nahuatl sign for movement can be found at the center of the Sun Stone or Aztec Calendar (formed by the glyphs of the four previous eras surrounding the Sun of the present era, *Ollin Tonatiuth,* "The Sun of Movement"); the Nahuatl word for "heart" is derived from it, *y-ollotl,* literally, "his mobility," as is *yoliliztli,* "life," the result of transforming motion.

Olmec. Mother culture of the Mesoamerican civilization; it refers to people "from the land of rubber."

Ololiuhqui. Name for medicinal herb whose seeds are round; from *ololihui,* "round like a ball"; it is used as an oracle in the *Tratado*; also known as *coaxiuth,* "snake herb"; it causes hallucinations.

Olpeyauque. (Ones-Overflowing-With-Rubber), in the *Tratado*, another metaphor for birds.

Oxomoco. (Turpentine-Ointment-Two-Pine-Torches), from *oxitl,* "turpentine ointment," *ome,* "two," and *ocotl,* "pine torches"; *ocote* is the stick of pine kindling; first man in the Mesoamerican primordial couple; in Nahuatl mythology, he is credited (together with his spouse, *Cipactonal),* with originating the divinatory arts. *Oxomoco* is also known as *Huehueh,* "Old Man," which at times is used as a metaphor for fire.

Petate. Straw mat used for sleeping; from *petatl,* "matting."

Peyote. Name of diverse kinds of cactaceous plants used for medicinal and spiritual purposes; its fruit or "button" has hallucinogenic properties; from *peyotl,* "a thing that glimmers, glows"; it is used as the main sacrament of the Native American Church, a Pan-Indian religious/spiritual movement which has extended throughout Native groups in North America.

Piciete. Common tobacco used by peasants; derived from *piztli,* "tiny," and *iyetl,* "tobacco."

Quetzalcoatl. (Plumed Serpent), God and cultural hero of a central myth and historic legend in Mexico and Yucatan, where he was known by his Mayan name, *Kukulcan; Quetzalcoatl* is a compound noun derived from *quetzalli,* "precious feather," and *coatl,* "snake"; he is identified with *Ehecatl,* the God of Wind, and with the planet Venus; as a Toltec cultural hero, *Ce-Acatl Topiltzin Quetzalcoatl,* (*Ce-Acatl,* "One Reed," is his calendaric name, whereas *Topiltzin* is formed by the prefix *to-,* "our," and *piltzin,* "lord"), he promised to return after being defeated by the priests of the new cult of *Tezcatlipoca;* Hernán Cortés was identified with this deity when he first appeared on the shores of the Aztec empire in 1519, the year *Ce-Acatl,* which was the date prophesied for the return of Lord *Quetzalcoatl.*

location of the main colonial administration for the Spanish empire overseas.

Siempre. Spanish for "always."

Tehuehuetl. (Stone Drum), from *tetl,* "stone," and *huehuetl,* "drum."

Temazcal. Mesoamerican sweat-lodge; derived from *temazcalli:* from *tema,* "to bathe," and *calli,* "house."

Temicxoch. (Dream-Flower), compound name from *temictl,* "dream," and *xochitl,* "flower."

Tenexiete. (Lime tobacco), from *tenextli,* "lime" (which is itself a compound noun formed by *tetl,* "stone," and *nextli,* "ash"), and *iyetl,* "tobacco"; it is ground *piciete* mixed with lime.

Teotihuacan. (Place of the Gods), from *teotl,* "god," and *huacan,* "place or surroudings"; one of the most important archeological zones in Mexico, site of the ancient religious and cultural center whose influence extended throughout Mesoamerica; there is evidence that it was sacked and burned around 650 A.D.

Tepeyollotli. (Heart of the Mountain), from *tepetl,* "mountain," and *yollotli,* "heart"; the jaguar *nahual* of *Tezcatlipoca;* also lord of all animals, and responsible for the echo and rumbles of the Earth.

Tezcatlipoca. (Smoking Mirror), the God of the sorcerers, also known as *Yaotl,* "The Warrior," and *Telpochtli,* "The Eternally Young"; originally, he symbolized the night sky, thus his name, "Smoking Mirror," from *tezcatl,* "mirror," and *ipoca,* "it emits smoke." A Mesoamerican legend tells how he, jealous of wise *Quetzalcoatl,* lured the good king into drunkenness and incest with his sister, *Xochiquetzal,* and then he showed him his face in the "mirror that smokes" and *Quetzalcóatl,* penitent for his guilt, migrated south and set to sea on a raft of rattlesnakes with the promise that he would return in the year *Ce-Acatl* ("1 Reed"), which was the year Hernán Cortés and his Spanish fleet arrived.

Tlacuilo. Scriber, painter who recorded the hieroglyphs and other symbols in the Nahuatl picture writing system.

Tlahui. (Red Ocre), it is one of the four *Tlazolteteo,* Goddesses of Love and Filth; this is also the name of *Yappan's* wife in the myth about the creation of scorpions (see "The Story of *Yappan*").

Tlaloc. (Rain God), from *tlalli,* "land," and *oc,* "one who lies."

Tlamacazqui. (Spirit, priest), it literally means "one who will give something"; in the *Tratado* it is the term for any power entity.

Tlalteuctli. (Ruler of the Earth), from *tlalli,* "land," *teuctli,* "lord"; in the *Tratado,* Ruiz de Alarcón identified this deity as Goddess of the Earth.

Tlatlauhqui. (Red); this color is usually associated with the north; *tatlahuic* is a variant of *tlatlauhqui.*

Tlazolteotl. (Love Goddess), from *tazotli,* "beloved," and *teotl,* "god, goddess"; the plural form is *Tlazolteteo,* "Love Goddesses."

Tlazolteteo. (Love Goddesses), from *tazotli,* "beloved," and *teteo,* "gods, goddesses," the plural of *teotl,* "god, goddess"; in the *Tratado* there are four deities associated with the Goddesses of Love and Filth: *Cuaton, Caxxoch, Tlahui,* and *Xapel.*

Tlazopilli. (Beloved Prince, Beloved Princess), a ritual name for corn; from *tlazotli,* "precious, beloved thing," and *pilli,* "nobleman, noblewoman."

Toltec. Nahuatl-speaking Indian group whose capital was *Tollan;* for later Indians in Mesoamerica, *toltecatl* signified "artist."

Tonacacihuatl. (Lady of Our Flesh), from the prefix *to-,* "our," *nacatl,* "flesh," "sustenance," and *cihuatl,* "woman"; another name for *Xochiquetzal;* it is also used in the *Tratado* as a ritual name for corn.

Tonal. (Soul, spirit), from the Nahuatl word *tonalli,* "sun-like," which is derived from the verb *tona,* "to shine, to be sunny, to be warm."

Tonalamatl. (Book or codex of days or destinies), compound name formed by *tonal,* "day," "destiny," "spirit," and *amatl,* "bark paper"; it was a book used for divination and as an astrological almanac.

Tonantzin. (Our Mother), from the prefix *to-,* "our," and *nantli,* "mother," together with the suffix *-tzin,* which indicates endearment and respect; Nahuatl name for the *Virgen de Guadalupe,* the patron saint of Mexico; in classical times, it was another name for *Centeotl,* the Corn Deity.

Tonatiuth. (Sun God), the name of the Fifth Sun in the Nahuatl creation myth.

Topan. (The Heaven), celestial realm, also called *ChiucnauhTopan* (from *chiuc-nahui,* "five-plus-four") because it had nine levels.

Verde. Spanish for "green."

Xapel. Name of one of the four Goddesses of Love and Filth, *Tlazolteteo.*

Xochipilli. (Flower-Lord), from *xochitl,* "flower," and *pilli,* "nobleman"; patron of festivities and poetry, and symbol of summer.

Xochiquetzal. (Flower-Plume), Love Goddess; from *xochitl,* "flower," and *quetzalli,* "precious plume"; Goddess of flowers, arts, and crafts; also known as *Tonacacihuatl* and *Chalchihuitlicue.*

Xochitl. (Flower), also the last day of the Mesoamerican 20-day month.

Xolotl. (The Double), name of the *Quetzalcoatl's* double; he is a god who appears in the *Tratado* in apposition to *Capanilli.*

Xoxouhqui. (Green), this color is usually associated with the west; *xoxo-huic* is a variant of *xoxouhqui.*

Yaotl. (The Warrior), another name for *Tezcatlipoca.*

Yappan. (Black-Corn-Flag), metaphorical name for the black scorpion.

Yauhtli. (Sweet marigold or anise), medicinal herb used for incense; from *iyauhtli,* "offering flower," and *iyahua,* "smoke offering."

Yayauhqui. (Dusky, dark in color); *yayahuic* is another variant of *yay-auhqui.*

Yoliliztli. (Life in Motion), from *yollotl,* "heart," which itself derives as *y-ollotl,* "his movement," from *ollin,* "movement," the principle of life.

Yolloxochitl. (Magnolia), from *yollotl,* "heart," and *xochitl,* "flower."

Yohuallahuantzin. (Night-Drinker), in classic times, another name for *Xipe ToTec,* a Fertility God.

Bibliography

Aguirre Beltrán, Gonzalo. *Medicina y magia: el proceso de aculturación en la estructura colonial.* Mexico City: Instituto Nacional Indigenista, Colección de Antropología Social, no. 1, 1963.

Andrews, J. Richard. *Introduction to Classical Nahuatl.* Austin: University of Texas, 1975.

———— and Ross Hassig, eds. and trans. *Treatise on the Heathen Superstitions That Today Live Among the Indians Native to This New Spain, 1629, by Hernando Ruiz de Alarcón.* Norman and London: University of Oklahoma Press, 1984.

Beck, Peggy V., Anna Lee Walters and Nia Francisco. *The Sacred: Ways of Knowledge, Sources of Life.* Flagstaff, Arizona: Navajo Community College Press, Northland Publishing Co., 1990.

Bierhorst, John. *A Nahuatl-English Dictionary and Concordance to the 'Cantares Mexicanos,' with an Analytic Transcription and Grammatical Notes.* Stanford, CA: Stanford University Press, 1985.

————. *Cantares Mexicanos: Songs of the Aztecs.* Translated from the Nahuatl with an Introduction and Commentary by John Bierhorst. Stanford, CA: Stanford University Press, 1985.

————. *Four Masterworks of American Indian Literature: Quetzalcoatl, the Ritual of Condolence, Cuceb, the Night Chant.* New York: Farrar, Straus & Giroux, 1974.

————. "On the Nature of Aztec Poetry," *Review 29*: 69–71. New York: Inter-American Relations, 1981.

————. *The Sacred Path: Spells, Prayers and Power Songs of the American Indian.* New York: Quille, 1983.

Brinyon, Daniel G. *Ancient Nahuatl Poetry.* New York: AMS Press, 1969. Reprint of the 1890 ed.; originally published in 1887.

Cabrera, Luis. *Diccionario de aztequismos.* Mexico City: Oasis, 1980.

Cardenal, Ernesto. *Quetzalcoatl.* Translated by Clifton Ross. Berkeley, CA: New Earth Publications, 1990.

Carrasco, David. *Quetzalcóatl and the Irony of Empire.* Chicago: University of Chicago Press, 1982.

Caso, Alfonso. *Los calendarios prehispánicos.* Mexico City: Universidad Nacional Autónoma de México (UNAM), Instituto de Investigaciones Históricas, 1967.

Coe, Michael D. and Gordon Whittaker, trans. and eds. *Aztec Sorcerers in Seventeenth Century Mexico: The Treatise on Superstitions by Hernando Ruiz de Alarcón.* Albany: State University of New York at Albany, Institute for Mesoamerican Studies, Publication no. 7, 1982.

Corpi, Lucha. *Variaciones sobre una tempestad / Variations on a Storm.* Berkeley, CA: Third Woman Press, 1990.

de Gerez, Toni. *2-Rabbit, 7-Wind: Poems from Ancient Mexico Retold from Nahuatl Texts.* New York: Viking, 1971.

Fellows, W. H. "The Treatises of Hernando Ruiz de Alarcón," *Tlalocan,* vol. 7: 309–55. Mexico City: UNAM, Instituto de Investigaciones Históricas, 1977.

Field, Frederick V. *Pre-Hispanic Mexican Stamp Designs*. New York, NY: Dover Publications, 1974.

Garibay K., Angel María. *Historia de la literatura náhuatl*, 2 vols. Mexico City: Editorial Porrúa, 1953–54.

González, Rafael J. "Symbol and Metaphor in Nahuatl Poetry," *ETC.: A Review of General Semantics*, vol. 25, no. 4, 1968.

Guerra, Fray Juan. *Arte de la lengua mexicana que fue usual entre los indios del obispado de Guadalajara y parte de los de Durango y Michoacán, escrito en 1692 por Fr. Juan Guerra, predicador y definidor de la Provincia de Franciscanos de Santiago de Jalisco*. 2nd ed. by Alberto Santoscoy. Guadalajara, Mexico: Imprenta Ancira y Hno. A. Ochoa, 1900.

Hinz, Eike. *Anthropologische Analyse altaztekischer Texte, Teil 1: Die magischen Texte im Tratado Ruiz de Alarcons*. Hamburg: Kommissionverl. Kalus Renner, 1970.

Horcasitas, Fernando. *The Aztecs Then and Now*. Mexico City: Minutiae Mexicana, 1974.

Karttunen, Frances. *An Analytical Dictionary of Nahuatl*. Austin: University of Texas Press, 1983.

Kissam, Edward. "Aztec Poems," *Antaeus* (New York), no. 4 (Winter 1971): 7–17.

———— and Michael Schimdt. *Flower and Song: Poems of the Aztec Peoples*. London: Anvil Press Poetry, 1977.

Lafaye, Jacques. *Quetzalcoatl and Guadalupe: The Formation of Mexican National Conciousness, 1531–1813*. Tr. Benjamin Keen. Chicago: University of Chicago Press, 1976.

Leander, Brigitta. *In xochitl in cuicatl: Flor y canto: La poesía de los aztecas*. Mexico City: Instituto Nacional Indigenista, 1972.

————. "La poesía náhuatl: función y carácter," *Etnologiska Studier*, 31: 1–62. Göteborg, Sweden: Göteborgs Etnografiska Museum, 1971.

León Portilla, Miguel. *Aztec Thought and Culture: A Study of the Ancient Nahuatl Mind*. Norman: University of Oklahoma Press, 1963.

————. *The Broken Spears: Aztec Account of the Conquest of Mexico*. Boston: Beacon Press, 1966.

————. *Trece poetas del mundo azteca*. Mexico City: Universidad Nacional Autónoma de Mexico, 1967.

————. *Native Mesoamerican Spirituality: Ancient Myths, Discourses, Stories, Doctrines, Hyms, Poems from the Aztec, Yucatec, Quiche-Maya and other Sacred Traditions*. New York: Paulist Press, 1980.

————. *Pre-Columbian Literatures of Mexico*. Norman: University of Oklahoma Press, 1968.

López Austin, Alfredo. "Conjuros médicos de los nahuas," *Revista de la Universidad de México*, vol. 24, no. 11, i–xvi, julio 1970.

————. "Conjuros nahuas del siglo XVII," *Revista de la Universidad de México*, vol. 27, no. 4, i–xvi, diciembre 1972.

————. "Cuarenta clases de magos del mundo náhuatl," *Estudios de Cultura Náhuatl,* vol. 7: 87–117, 1968.

————. "Términos del nahuallatolli," *Historia Mexicana,* vol. 17, no. 1, julio–septiembre 1967: 1–36.

————. *Textos de medicina náhuatl.* Mexico City: UNAM, Instituto de Investigaciones Históricas, 1975.

Macazaga Ordoño, César. *Diccionario de la lengua náhuatl.* Mexico City: Editorial Innovación, 1979.

Mönnich, Anneliese. "La supervivencia de antiguas representaciones indígenas en la religión popular de los nawas de Veracruz y Puebla." In Luis Reyes García and Dieter Christensen, eds., *Der Ring aus Tlalocan: Mythen und Gebete, Lieder und Erzählungen der heutigen Nahhua in Veracruz und Pueblo, Mexico / El Anillo de Tlalocan: mitos, oraciones, cantos y cuentos de los nawas actuales en los Estados de Veracruz y Puebla, México.* Berlin: Gebr. Mann Verland, 1976: 139–44.

Nicholson, Irene. *Firefly in the Night: A Study of Ancient Mexican Poetry and Symbolism.* London: Faber and Faber, 1959.

Paso y Troncoso, Francisco del. *La botánica entre los nahuas y otros estudios.* Pilar Márquez, ed. Mexico City: Secretaría de Educación Pública, 1988.

————, ed. Ruiz de Alarcón: "Tratado de las supersticiones y costumbres gentílicas que oy viven entre los indios naturales desta Nueva España," *Anales del Museo Nacional de México,* vol. 6, 1892: 125–223.

————, ed. Ruiz de Alarcón: "Tratado de las supersticiones y costumbres gentílicas que oy viven entre los indios naturales desta Nueva España." In Jacinto de la Serna et al., notes and introduc tion by Francisco del Paso y Troncoso, *Tratado de las idolatrías, supersticiones, dioses, ritos, hechicerías y otras costumbres gentílicas de las razas aborígenes de México,* 2 vols. Mexico City: Navarro, Ediciones Fuente Cultural, 1953–54, vol. 2: 17–180.

Ponce, Pedro. "Breve relación de los dioses y ritos de la gentilidad," *Anales del Museo Nacional de México,* vol. 6, 1892: 3–11.

————. "Brief Relation of the Gods and Rites of Heathenism." In J. Richard Andrews and Ross Hassig, trans. and eds., *Treatise on the Heathen Superstitions That Today Live Among the Indians Native to This New Spain, 1629, by Hernando Ruiz de Alarcón.* Norman and London: University of Oklahoma Press, 1984: 211–18.

Quezada, Noemí. *Amor y magia amorosa entre los aztecas: supervivencia en el México colonial.* Mexico City: UNAM, Instituto de Investigaciones Antropológicas, 1975.

Ruiz de Alarcón, Hernando. *Aztec Sorcerers in Seventeeth Century Mexico: The Treatise on Superstitions by Hernando Ruiz de Alarcón.* Coe, Michael D. and Gordon Whittaker, trans. and eds. Albany: State University of New York at Albany, Institute for Mesoamerican Studies, Publication no. 7, 1982.

————. "Tratado de las supersticiones y costumbres gentílicas que hoy viven entre los indios naturales desta Nueva España," *Anales del Museo Nacional de México,* vol. 6, 1892: 125–223.

————. "Tratado de las supersticiones y costumbres gentílicas que hoy viven entre los indios naturales desta Nueva España." In Jacinto de la Serna et al., notes and introduction by Francisco del Paso y Troncoso, *Tratado de las idolatrías, supersticiones, dioses, ritos, hechicerías y otras costumbres gentílicas de las razas aborígenes de México,* 2 vols. Mexico City: Navarro, Ediciones Fuente Cultural, 1953–54, vol. 2: 17–180.

————. "Tratado de las supersticiones y costumbres gentílicas que hoy viven entre los indios naturales desta Nueva España." In Pedro Ponce, Pedro Sánchez de Aguilar et al. *El alma encantada: Anales del Museo Nacional de México. Presentación de Fernando Benítez.* Mexico City: Instituto Nacional Indigenista / Fondo de Cultura Económica, 1987: 123–224. (Facsimilar edition of *Anales del Museo Nacional de México,* vol. 6, 1892).

————. *Treatise on the Heathen Superstitions That Today Live Among the Indians Native to this New Spain, 1629, by Hernando Ruiz de Alarcón.* J. Richard and Ross Hassig, trans. and eds. Norman and London: University of Oklahoma Press, 1984.

Sandoval, Rafael. *Arte de la lengua mexicana. Prólogo y notas de Alfredo López Austin.* Mexico City: UNAM, Instituto de Investigaciones Históricas, 1965.

Sawyer-Lauçanne, Christopher. *The Destruction of the Jaguar: Poems from the Books of Chilam Balam.* San Francisco: City Lights Books, 1987.

Séjourné, Laurette. *Burning Water: Thought and Religion in Ancient Mexico.* London: Thames and Hudson, 1957.

————. *El pensamiento náhuatl cifrado por los calendarios.* Mexico City: Siglo XXI, 1981.

————. *El universo de Quetzalcóatl.* Mexico City: Fondo de Cultura Económica, 1962.

Serna, Jacinto de la. "Manual de ministros de indios para el conocimiento de sus idolatrías, y extirpación de ellas," *Anales del Museo Nacional de México,* vol. 6, 1892: 261–480.

Siméon, Rémi. *Diccionario de la lengua náhuatl o mexicana.* Translated by Josefina Oliva de Coll. Mexico City: Siglo XXI, 1977.

————. *Dictionnaire de la langue nahuatl ou mexicaine.* Graz, Austria: Akademische Druck & Verlagsanstalt, 1963. Reprint of the 1885 ed.

Spence, Lewis. *Arcane Secrets and Occult Lore of Mexico and Mayan Central America.* London: Rider & Co., 1930.

Villanueva, Tino. *Crónica de mis años peores.* La Jolla, CA: Lalo Press, 1987.

Wasson, R. Gordon et al. *María Sabina and her Mazatec Mushroom Velada.* New York and London: Harcourt Brace Jovanovich, 1974.

Waters, Frank. *Mexico Mystique: The Coming Sixth World of Consciousness.* Chicago: The Swallow Press, 1989. Reprint of the 1975 ed.